BET ON A BILLIONAIRE

SERIES BY NELLIE STEELE

BET ON A BILLIONAIRE

A CLEAN BILLIONAIRE ROMANCE

HEARTS AND HOLDINGS
BOOK ONE

NELLIE STEELE

A Novel Idea Publishing

Books with Character

CHAPTER 1

GRANT

$\mathcal{H}$ is pulse pounded as he stared out over the glowing New Orleans cityscape, each light a testament to his life's work. The air in the penthouse was thick with tension, the silence only broken by the occasional *clink* of ice in his attorney's glass. Fiddling with his diamond cufflinks, he gritted his teeth.

"I'm sorry, Grant," a deep voice said from behind him.

Grant twisted to face him, his chiseled jaw tight. "You should be. How could you have let this happen?"

"No one could have seen this coming. No one."

"You're here because you see things coming no one else could." His back muscles tightened as he leaned over to grip the edge of the polished mahogany desk.

Mitchell winced after a sip of his brandy. "Grant–"

"Don't patronize me, Mitchell. Fix this. That's what I pay you for."

The old man ran a hand through his silver hair before he

adjusted the button on his expensive suit and eased into a seat on the opposite side of the desk. "I'm not sure there is an easy fix to this, Grant."

The crystal paperweight rattled as Grant slammed his hands on the desk. He flung a finger back toward the floor-to-ceiling window of the penthouse office of the Harrington Global Enterprises. "Do you see those lights? The millions of them? They can be seen from space; that's how many of them there are."

Mitchell let his features settle into a neutral position as he braced for the tongue-lashing. After twenty-five years with the energy and telecommunication powerhouse, he'd lived through more than enough of Grant Harrington's outbursts.

"I provide the energy for every single one of those lights. When someone makes a call, it's because of this company."

"I'm well-aware of what this company does."

"My company." He poked a finger at his broad chest. "My company provides power and communication for the eastern seaboard, from Florida to Boston."

Mitchell lifted his chin as he swung an ankle onto his knee, carefully balancing the red-tabbed folder on his lap. "Unfortunately, that may no longer be the case, Grant. I'm sorry, but the board has serious concerns about your ability to successfully manage and grow this company."

Grant frowned as he spun away from the sparsely furnished, modern office to face the window again. He'd taken the reins of the small company of Harrington Holdings from his grandfather and father twenty-five years ago as a young man.

He'd spent his life growing that small but thriving company into a global powerhouse, thrusting the Harringtons from well-off to commanding. He'd lost four wives in the pursuit of his ambitions with Harrington Global. The weight of generations pressed on his shoulders. This company wasn't just profit; it was legacy. A testament to the Harringtons of the past, and the generations to come.

But the bottom line he'd built had kept investors happy, and his latest spouse in the lap of luxury. To lose everything he'd built was a slap in the face from every board member who'd called his abilities into question.

Grant heaved a sigh, crossing his arms. "Are you sure we don't have the votes?"

"Doesn't seem that way. Only Blackburn, Mitchell, Foster, and Whitfield are sure votes your way."

Grant rubbed the back of his neck as the other names rambled through his mind. Was there anyone's arm he could twist to swing the vote?

"Not Dunbar?"

"No, and he's only the fifth vote. We need a super majority for a vote of no confidence. With Dunbar, we don't even have a majority."

Grant flicked his gaze to the ceiling as he shook his head. "Who started this?"

"Does it matter?"

He snapped his gaze to the attorney. He wanted a name. He needed to identify his enemy before he formed an attack plan.

"What do you think?"

Mitchell flicked the folder closed. "James McAllister with the support of Veronica Lawson."

"That figures. McAllister's been after me since he landed that position on the board. My father never should have trusted him."

"Favors were owed. That's how debts were settled."

He seethed as he faced the fact that a favor from a bygone generation could cost him everything. "Those debts are costing me big."

"Unless you can find a way to work around this, they're

going to cost you this company. The standards set forth are clear. Clean up your image, or relinquish the reins at Harrington Global." Mitchell slid the folder onto the polished wood before he snapped his briefcase, lying on the chair next to him, shut and rose. He fiddled with his button as he lifted his attache case. "The vote comes at the next board meeting. That gives us some time, but not much."

Grant's nostrils flared as he heard the words he didn't want to hear.

"Goodnight, Grant."

Grant slid his eyes closed as frustration tightened his jaw again. "Goodnight, Mitchell."

The lithe man strode to the door, hesitating in the doorway as he glanced back at the fifty-year-old billionaire. "We'll talk tomorrow, Grant. Maybe we can come up with a play."

"I expect us to. I don't pay all those billable hours to be defeated by a coup."

The man strode from the space into the quiet corporate offices, long since abandoned at this late hour by any other workers.

Grant stared out the window for another moment before he swiveled the thick leather office chair around and sank into the supple leather.

It creaked as it molded to his body, still fit for fifty. He let his head fall back against the high back. The news was not what he'd hoped. Rumblings of a takeover had been quietly whispered at the water cooler and restrooms. But that had happened before. Nothing had come from it.

Grant Harrington was not a man to be trifled with. Except this time, someone had managed to whip enough board members into a frenzy over his image and how it affected the company.

He let his forehead sink into his hand with a deep sigh.

He'd maneuvered out of tight spots before. Could he pull it off again?

With a deep sigh, he dragged himself from his chair to the wet bar across the office and poured himself a whiskey. He sipped it before returning to his seat to stare over the empire he'd built.

The room felt colder as the reality of the situation sunk in. Grant had always been a pillar, unyielding in the face of adversity. But now, as the empire he built threatened to crumble, a rare flicker of fear crossed his stoic visage.

His jaw tightened again before he launched the glass across the room. It shattered against the far wall, scattering bits of glass across the floor.

"Whoa. Bad day at work?" a voice asked.

Grant spun to face the door, finding his daughter, Sierra, poking her head inside. "Something like that."

The twenty-four-year-old pushed her way inside with a chuckle as she flicked a lock of highlighted blonde hair over her shoulder. "Nothing the Great Grant Harrington can't handle, though, right?"

He didn't answer, not tearing his eyes away from the cityscape as she poured two drinks at the bar and sauntered toward him. She held one glass out toward him before perching on the edge of the desk.

He snatched it from her hands and sipped it. She crossed her bare legs at the ankle, swinging her designer five-inch-heeled pumps back and forth.

"Another new pair of shoes?" Grant asked.

"I may have done a little retail therapy earlier. Things are...stressful at work." She sipped her brandy before she toggled on the camera of her phone and studied her face. She puckered her red lips before she fixed a smudge of her thick eyeliner. "I should schedule a facial or something. I look tired."

Grant loosened his tie and undid the buttons on his collar. "New toy I bought you not working out?"

She leapt off the desk to pace around the room, her tight pencil skirt forcing her to walk with one foot in front of the other as she toyed with the giant bow on her polka-dotted blouse. "I'm just up to my ears in reviewing everything. The last person mismanaged it so badly, it'll take a miracle to pull it back into the black."

Grant pressed his lips together as she vented. His daughter had grown up in the lap of luxury. She'd never survive their fall from grace.

"But I'll get it back on track. Count on that. I've got ideas brewing already. They came to me after the fifth pair of shoes I bought. Oh, by the way, I may have maxed out the card. Be a dear and clear the balance, would you?"

"Yep," he answered.

She planted a kiss on his cheek and patted his shoulder. "Thanks, Daddy."

She stood, biting into her blood-red lip as she swiveled a heel against the floor.

"Something else you need, Sierra?"

"Just wondering why there's a limit on that card anyway? I feel like I'm eighteen. Can't you just make a call and nix the limit?"

"It's there for a reason, kid."

"But that's the thing, Daddy, I'm not a kid anymore. I mean, I'm running an entire publishing company. And doing a damn good job at it, too."

That I bought you.

"Oh, by the way, I'm thinking of renaming it something catchier than Heritage Publishing." She rolled her eyes as she stuck a hand on her hip.

Grant tightened his grip on the glass before he sipped his drink again. He had bigger problems than what trendy name his daughter would give to the publishing company he'd bought her for her birthday when she'd complained she was bored.

She babbled on about something or another, while his troubles continued to flit through his mind.

"Daddy!" Sierra's sharp voice demanded a moment later.

He twisted to find her hands on her hips, her blonde curls bouncing as she tilted her head. "Are you even listening to me?"

"Of course I am."

She narrowed her eyes as she crossed her arms. "Then what did I say?"

"You're changing everything at the publishing company, and it's going to be great." He raised his eyebrows at her. "See, I was listening."

"That's hardly the perfect summary. You haven't been listening at all. What's wrong with you?"

"A little trouble with the board. Nothing I can't handle."

He sipped his drink without taking his eyes off New Orleans. He didn't want to betray his unease. Mitchell's unsettled attitude set him on edge. They'd weathered many storms together, and the normally unflappable Mitchell seemed worried.

"I'm not convinced. What's going on?"

He slid his eyes sideways over the rim of his glass before he rose to refill his drink. "I told you, nothing I can't handle."

"Yeah, not buying it." Sierra plopped in his chair and picked up the crystal paperweight, tossing it from hand to hand. "Tell me what's going on."

"It's nothing to worry about, Princess. I'll handle it." Grant slid a hand into his pocket, hoping she'd be distracted into returning to talking about her favorite subject: herself.

"You just threw a glass across the room and broke it into a

million pieces. You're obviously distracted. I'm worried no matter what you say."

"You shouldn't worry, you'll get wrinkles. And I don't want to pay for a facelift in your twenties."

Sierra shot him an unimpressed glance. "You can't hide behind humor. What was Mitchell Caldwell doing in your office at this time of night that made you throw a glass across the room after he left?"

Grant stalked across the room and collapsed onto the leather couch, running his hands through his dirty blond hair. "Little problem with the board."

She arched an eyebrow, prodding him to continue. Her features slid from light to serious in an instant. He spotted the familiar shrewd businesswoman he'd trained emerge.

He rolled his tongue in his mouth as he tried to form the words for the unbelievable situation that would lead to his ousting from his own company. "A vote of no confidence unless I can improve my image."

"But you have the votes, right?"

He swung an ankle onto his knee. "Mitchell says no."

Sierra's lips tugged into a pout, and her eyes fell onto the red-tabbed folder. "Is this his report?"

He bobbed his head up and down. She may as well take a gander at it now and resign herself to the fall they'd take as a family.

Sierra flicked it open with a manicured nail and scanned it before she scoffed. "An image not befitting a CEO of a global corporation? Project a more stable, family-friendly persona? Are they serious?"

"Apparently," Grant answered.

She pouted her red lips as she perused the paper again. "Is this even legal? How can they hold this against you if you make them money?"

"It's legal. The company's brand is at their discretion. And according to McAllister, I don't fit that."

Sierra drummed the white tips of her fake nails against the desk, staring into space.

Grant rose from his seat and poured another drink. "Say goodbye to Harrington Global, Sierra. I'll do my best to keep your publishing company out of their hands."

She slapped her palm against the desk. "No."

He glanced over his shoulder at her. "A temper tantrum isn't going to fix this, honey."

"We can fix this."

"I'm afraid not. We have less than sixty days before this vote. I'm not going to reform my image that fast in a way they'll believe."

Sierra rose from the seat and leaned against the desk, kicking one foot over the other. "Yes, we can."

Grant raised his eyebrows at her. What was she up to?

"You forget, Daddy. I am obsessed with image. I'm all about image. Have you seen my Insta posts? They are all perfectly branded. Like, now that I've taken over the publishing company, I wear glasses to look more like a publisher."

"A new suit and a pair of glasses aren't going to fix this."

"No, but I know what will. I have an idea. And it can't fail. We need to find you a wife."

"Sierra, I can't just pick up a woman tonight and marry her."

"Of course not." Sierra let out a scornful chuckle and rolled her eyes. "We need to pick someone to help your image." She grabbed her phone and tapped on it. "Leave it to me, Daddy. I've got this. You'll have your pick of women."

Grant stared at her, his features crinkled, finding the idea bizarre, even desperate. But desperate times called for desperate measures.

Sierra enthusiastically typed on her phone, but Grant couldn't help feeling a niggling doubt. Was this really the best way to save his empire?

* * *

Grant stared at the long line of women as he slumped in the booth at the nightclub. In the cold light of day, the place didn't look nearly as appealing as when it glittered and glowed at night. Neither did the women in the line, who he was certain all would look better in the dim light of a bar.

Sierra shuffled through a few papers as she set up shop next to him.

"This is a horrible idea, Sierra."

"It's not. It's fine. There are hundreds of women here. We just need to pick one, offer her a contract to stay married to you for a year - and voila! You've got a brand new family-man image to appease the board." She took a red pen and scanned a paper, making a few notes.

Grant stared at the long line of similar-looking faces. Tanned, sculpted, bleached-blonde, made-up. "There isn't one woman in that line who screams 'family-friendly.' It looks like the line-up for the next lingerie model."

"Trust me, Daddy," Sierra said, patting his hand. "There's got to be someone here who will fit the bill. Here, look at this one…" She pointed at a paper with her pen. "Candi loves animals and yoga, along with exotic travel."

Grant checked the application number before he scanned the group of women wearing ID badges marked with numbers. "Candi also looks like she's made of plastic. Sierra, this is not going to work."

"Daddy, you hired an image consultant, and I'm here to solve your problems. With my degrees in public relations,

I've got this. Let me do my work." She swiped her phone from the table and tapped on it for a moment.

He opened his mouth to tell her he hadn't hired her. He hadn't asked for her help. In less than twenty-four hours, Sierra had cobbled together an interview process to pick a wife. With a five-million-dollar payout for the woman who would help him win back his company, the call for help had brought out every gold digger in the city limits.

He settled back in his seat, with his arms crossed. Face after endless face paraded in front of him, flashing smiles, winks, and cleavage in an attempt to win the prize: one year of marriage and five million dollars.

After a while, they all looked alike. As the line dwindled, so did Grant's hopes for surviving the attack on his company. None of these women would work. None of them could be trusted. And none of them would improve his image.

As the last woman rose, rubbing her hand seductively across his hand with a wink, he let out a long sigh, tossing his pen in the air. "Well, that's that. There goes the company."

"Wait," Sierra said. "I think I've got the winner right here."

CHAPTER 2

JULIA

*H*er knee bounced as she waited for the printer to spit out the last pages of her manuscript. The rhythmic hum and occasional *clank* of the printer filled the small closet-turned office. Julia bit into her lower lip as she collected the warm pages, still smelling of fresh ink, that ended one chapter.

She pounded the edges of the manuscript against the worn wooden desk, surrounded by towering stacks of books and scribbled-upon notepads in the cramped, dimly lit room that served as her writing haven.

Her phone chimed, reminding her of the upcoming meeting with her new publisher. Just as she'd finished her sixth manuscript, the company she'd worked for changed hands. The new owner cleaned house, sending out an email on her first day as CEO telling them everyone and everything was under review.

Payments were frozen, and manuscripts were being re-

12

reviewed. Some authors would be cut. She prayed she wasn't one of them. She'd expected to receive her advance three weeks ago, but it hadn't come because of the transition.

Instead, she'd been summoned to a meeting. At least she'd made the shortlist for remaining on the roster of authors Heritage Publishing would continue to work with.

She stretched a binder clip around the manuscript and snapped it shut before she shoved the book draft into her fraying canvas tote before she dashed from the tiny office into her living room-kitchen combo. The compact space blended coziness and functionality with its well-worn but comfortable furniture. She dumped the bag on the small, round table that doubled as her dining table and prep area.

The television, framed by Victorian watercolors, blared a news report as she grabbed what remained of her smoothie. She flicked her gaze to the screen as she downed the last of her drink.

A stern-faced reporter stood outside a towering glass and steel edifice brandished with the bold blues and greens of the Harrington Global logo.

"The boardroom's bad boy on the brink? Rumors continue to swirl that Grant Harrington will soon be ousted as CEO of Harrington Global. The stunning news comes as questions crop up about mismanagement and ethics. Our reporter caught up with Harrington Global board member James McAllister for a statement."

Julia's fingers tightened around the smoothie cup, the coldness of the plastic seeping through to her skin as she watched the news unfold on screen.

"I think some of the board has had enough of Grant Harrington playing fast and loose with employees and the people he serves in this area and beyond," a man wearing an expensive suit said. "The fact is, the numbers show–"

The ringing of her cell phone interrupted the man's

words. Julia glanced at the display as she aimed the remote at the television and switched it off.

Her sister's name glowed on the screen. She swiped to accept the call and pressed the phone to her ear, balancing it with her shoulder as she washed her cup. "Hey, sis."

"Hi, Juju," her sister, Alicia, said. "How's life in the big city?"

Julia rolled her eyes at the affectionate nickname used by most of her friends and family. "Interesting."

"What does that mean?"

"It means this publisher change has been harder on me than I realized."

Alicia clicked her tongue on the other end of the line. "Hang in there. They'd be crazy to get rid of you. Your writing is superb."

Julia dumped the clean cup in the dish drainer and wiped her hands on a towel. "Yeah, well, superb or not, it may not be provocative enough for this new owner. And besides, you can't comment; you're my sister. You'll lie."

"I don't lie, sis. I'm a cop, remember?"

"Yeah, in a tiny town in Maine. The most you do is write tickets when someone does thirty-five on Main Street."

"Hey, watch it. I wasn't always a cop in a sleepy town in Maine."

Julia smiled as she hurried to her bedroom. "Yeah, yeah, you were a rough and tumble agent with the FBI. I still can't believe you left that job to go back to Harbor Cove."

"Just because you left, doesn't mean we all hate it."

Julia tugged on one of her riding boots over her jean leggings and zipped it up before she tapped to turn on her speakerphone and dumped the phone next to her as she worked on the other boot.

"I didn't hate it there. You know that."

"Yeah, I know the reason you left."

Julia's mind flitted to it before she shoved the painful memory aside. She needed to focus. She needed to stay on the company's payroll so she had more time to avoid home.

"Anyway, I need to get going before I'm late to meet my publisher."

"Good luck, Juju. Just remember, you can always come home if it doesn't work out."

Julia frowned at the phone, wrapping an infinity scarf around her neck and fluffing the autumn-leaf-covered fabric. "Thanks, Alicia. Bye."

She jabbed at the phone to end the call before she gripped the dresser's edge and blew out a long sigh. The loss of this job would leave her with few options, and she couldn't go home.

She slid her eyes shut as she centered herself. She had no room for error. She'd nail this. Her writing was good. No, her writing was great. She had to go into this meeting with that attitude. She couldn't flinch.

Julia opened her eyes and stared in the mirror, running a hand through her shoulder-length brunette hair. It fell back into place in its simple but chic cut.

"You got this."

She offered herself a nod, staring at her own blue eyes. A second later, she rolled them. "Who am I kidding? She's going to eat me alive."

Julia collapsed on the edge of her bed and ran a quick Internet search for tips for introverts to sell themselves. After scanning the advice she'd seen a dozen times before, she began the rehearsal of her conversation with the publisher.

She'd done it a dozen times already, and the conversation would never go the way she expected. But it eased her nerves to practice what she hoped to say.

She rose and fussed with her scarf for another minute

before she hurried from her bedroom, grabbed the tote bag with her manuscript, swung it and her nondescript purse over her shoulder, and darted out the door.

"On your way out?" her elderly neighbor asked as she locked her door behind her.

"Oh, hi, Mrs. Grayson, yes. Wish me luck. I'm dropping off my manuscript with the new publisher."

"Oh, you don't need luck, dear. You're an excellent writer." The woman slicked a lock of blue-gray hair behind her ears. "If they don't see that, they're fools."

"Thanks for the vote of confidence," Julia said, with a smile. Unfortunately, fools or not, she'd be the one with the issue if she didn't get this job. Without a paycheck, she wouldn't make her rent.

She raced down the hall, taking the stairs instead of the elevator. With a glance at her phone's display before she shoved it into the front pocket of her purse, she realized she'd be early for the coffee shop meeting.

It didn't matter. She'd rather be early than late. She could sit on pins and needles there rather than at home.

She stepped into the warm fall day, the heels of her boots clicking along the pavement as she pushed her way through the crowd.

With her phone back in her hand, she double-checked the address of the swanky coffee house over a dozen times as she navigated the route she'd memorized a week ago when the meeting had been set.

She swung the door open to the upscale coffee bar. The scent of roasted grounds and cinnamon smacked her in the face as she entered and scanned the half-empty room.

Her eyebrows pinched together as she searched the few faces for the new publishing company head.

Not here yet, she concluded as she sidled up to the counter and ordered a hot chocolate before settling into a corner seat, where she could easily keep an eye on the door.

She pressed a hand against the manuscript in her bag, her mind going over each plot point and second-guessing it. Maybe she should have made her female main character more aggressive. Or maybe she should have added more romance.

She sipped the hot beverage, cursing under her breath as she burned her tongue on it. It served as the perfect answer to her last notion. She couldn't add more romance to the book. Write what you know, they said. And she did not know much about that.

With a sigh, she checked the time on her phone for the umpteenth time. Five after the hour. Her publisher was late.

Not surprising, she thought, waiting as the time ticked by minute by minute. By quarter-after, she typed out and deleted a text to the woman a dozen times. Five minutes later, she finally decided to send an email that asked if she'd gotten the address wrong.

She set her phone on the table and drummed her fingers against her thigh as she stared at it, waiting for a response.

Her phone chimed a full eleven minutes later. She snatched it, her heart thudding, and read the response.

Whoops! I double-booked. So sorry! Can you drop by the Luxe Lounge on Prestige before noon?

Julia crinkled her brow as she stared at the message. If she wasn't mistaken, the Luxe Lounge was a glitzy nightclub, and also not open this time of the morning. What in the world was her publisher doing at a closed nightclub?

"Probably buying it," she murmured to herself as she mapped out her route and checked the time before typing a response that she would see the woman soon.

She collected her things, tossed her half-empty cup, and

hurried through the streets of New Orleans to the new meeting location.

She stared up at the big letters announcing the nightclub's name, currently unlit and dull. Women streamed from the building. She stood aside, allowing several to leave before she ducked inside.

"Oh, good morning," a bubbly blonde said as she ducked past the velvet curtain separating the lobby from the club's space.

She stepped in front of her, stopping any forward progress. "Here for an interview?"

"Ah," Julia hesitated, heat rising into her cheeks as she fumbled with her manuscript. "Yes. I have my manuscript right here."

The woman gave her a polite smile and nod as she thrust a paper toward her and grabbed a pen from a cup on a high table. "Fill this out, and we'll be with you in a minute. You're lucky, most of the crowd's gone now. You should get right in."

Crowd? How many writers was this woman interviewing for the few spots she'd offer? Too many, her mind concluded, as she filled in the necessary identifying information and moved on to the free response question section.

Her brow furrowed as she filled out the information, wondering what her likes, dislikes, and hobbies had to do with her manuscript's chances.

Probably has to do with how marketable I am as an author.

She jotted down as much as she could before she stuffed the pen back into the cup and slid the paper off the table.

The blonde flitted past, batting her obviously false eyelashes at Julia as she yanked the paper from her hands. "I'll get this right up to them."

"Thanks." Julia eased onto the edge of a purple velvet booth, the plush fabric soft against her palm.

She stared at the few people still milling around as self-doubt crept into her. She couldn't help feeling out of place. All the other women in the room were dressed to the nines in elegant fashions.

She tightened her grip on her tote bag as her palm turned sweaty against her jean-clad thigh. She glanced to the front, spotting the publisher in similar attire. The woman scanned an application with her sultry, smoky eyes before she slid the paper to someone sitting next to her. The high back of the curved booth blocked her view from spotting the individual.

With a sigh, she fought to stop the tickle in the back of her throat caused by the scent of expensive perfume that lingered in the air. She snapped her gaze to a trio of giggling women across the room, each with sleek, styled hair and makeup that looked like it had taken hours to perfect.

She glanced down at her own modest attire, suddenly regretting the simplistic style. Her tunic top and stretchy jeggings seemed dowdy amidst the sea of silk, satin, and skin. Her lack of elaborate makeup and false eyelashes made her minimal makeup seem nonexistent.

She shifted her legs back instinctively as a woman with a plunging neckline and barely-there skirt shrugged past Julia, with a confident stride that looked as rehearsed as her smile, which failed to reach her eyes.

Her pulse quickened as she felt like a fish out of water in the den of glamour. Her wholesome image would never fit into this world. She slid a hand down the bag, feeling the weight of her manuscript inside. Crafted with dedication, and not sculpted with rouge and revealing fabric, she struggled with the realization that she may leave this meeting with nothing. And if she did, she could kiss her dreams goodbye.

More than her dreams, she'd have nothing left. No job, no money. Nothing.

CHAPTER 3

GRANT

Stretching his neck to ease the crick, Grant's hopes faded fast. With the slew of women they'd interviewed, he thought they might find one suitable candidate. But it had been a bust. Which meant so were his chances at maintaining control of Harrington Global.

"Just forget it, Sierra, I'm finished."

"Uhhh," she said, her blue eyes darting back and forth, "so is Harrington Global unless we find you someone who will work."

"We'll find another way." He scanned the sea of sequins, false eyelashes, plumped lips, and extensions. "This is never going to work. These women aren't going to save my image; they're going to make it worse."

"I'm not sure it can get any worse than the time you married your secretary for six months."

Grant's hand flew to his temple, massaging away the

bitter memories of the failed marriage starting with a lack of common interests and ending with an affair on her part and subsequent fallout.

"That was a mistake."

"Obviously. Especially after we found out her brother was in the Mexican mob." Sierra held the sheet further away from her as she twirled the pen between her thumb and forefinger.

"And so is this," Grant huffed. The doubts he'd experienced last night when Sierra proposed the idea cropped up again. With the pool of candidates he'd seen today, putting a ring on any of their fingers would worsen his image, not to mention the ethical ramifications.

"No, I think we may have a good one here. Just one more. Come on, Daddy, don't be a defeatist."

He slumped back in the chair. "I'm not being a defeatist, but I don't have time for this nonsense. I need to call Mitchell and have a discussion about what it may take to stave off this blatant power grab. Maybe we can find something in McAllister's past."

"I'm telling you, we're not going to need to do that. I've got the winner right here." Sierra grinned as she checked off a few things on the paper and glanced up at the woman who had just handed in her application.

She narrowed her made-up eyes at the brunette. The woman looked uncomfortable as she studied a set of blonde bombshells who chatted across the club, their designer bags hanging from their forearms as they did the typical purse hold common when hoping to show off one's bag.

She adjusted the strap on her modest little tote bag before she ran her hands down her jeggings. She wasn't even wearing heels. The little wedge on her riding boots didn't count.

The woman's simply cut brunette hair fell to her shoulders, framing her mostly natural face. Sierra squinted. Was she even wearing a slick of mascara, or were those doe eyes natural?

She couldn't have looked more wholesome if she was a glass of whole milk. She was perfect. Maybe a little too perfect.

Sierra glanced down at the paper again. *Loves animals, reading, writing. Tries to listen to all sides of an argument and understand before tackling a problem. Meets adversity head-on.*

She smiled at the answers. The woman hadn't listed shopping, designers, exotic travel, caviar, champagne, and other expensive items, like the others. If they could check out a few more angles, they may have their savior.

With a satisfied smile, she flicked her gaze back to the woman and called her name. "Julia Stanton!"

The woman blew out a long breath as she rose. A scantily clad blonde stepped in front of her just as she started forward. She bounced back a step, allowing the woman to cross before she strode forward again.

As she eased into the seat across from them, she offered a genuine but nervous smile. "Hello."

Sierra studied her up close before she slid her eyes sideways to her father.

Grant sat straighter as the woman slid the straps of her unremarkable bag from her shoulder. This woman looked nothing like the others. She appeared intelligent, respectable, and honest. And she wasn't bad to look at either. Even though she wasn't slathered in make-up, bathed in perfume, wearing fake nails, or a designer outfit, she had a simple beauty he hadn't seen in a long time.

He glanced at the paper his daughter slid toward him, realizing now why she'd declared this woman a winner. She must have spotted her walking in. He scanned the answers. Hope bloomed in him that this crazy plan might just work.

"So, ah, Julia, is it?"

"Yes, that's right," she said, with a nod.

"It says here you enjoy reading and writing," he read before he flicked his gaze to her, trying to gauge if her response was honest.

She swallowed hard as she nodded. "Uh, yes. I actually have–"

"Yeah, we'll get to all that." Sierra cut off her response with a wave of her hand. "Are you really as virtuous as you look?"

The woman snapped her gaze to Sierra, her eyebrows pinching together and pretty features showing signs of confusion.

Grant let out a quiet laugh as he leaned forward with his award-winning smile. "What Sierra is trying to say is–"

"Is exactly what I said," Sierra interrupted. "Have you ever been convicted of a felony?"

"No," Julia answered, with a shake of her head.

"No felonies at all? Tax evasion, fraud, kidnapping, murder, nothing?" Sierra ticked them off on her fingers.

"Certainly not."

Grant opened his mouth to ask another question when Sierra continued. "Misdemeanors?"

Julia drew her chin back to her chest. "Uh, no."

Sierra flicked her eyebrows up. "Really? Nothing? DUI? Parking ticket? Speeding ticket?"

"No, none of those." The woman bit into the side of her lower lip as she slicked a lock of hair behind her ear.

Sierra jotted a note on the paper and slid it sideways toward Grant.

Love her!!!

Grant felt a rare flicker of optimism. Julia's presence alone might just be enough to sway the board's critical eye.

He'd spent years sizing up people in an instant before

making shrewd business decisions, and his intuition told him she was a good bet. He liked her, which would make this charade all the more believable.

He glanced at his gloating daughter and gave her a subtle nod.

"Well," she said, clasping her hands in front of her on the table, "it looks like you're a perfect fit for us."

The woman's lips turned up at the corners, though she seemed surprised. "Really? Don't you even want to see my manuscript?"

Grant's pleasant expression slipped as he pinched his eyebrows. What was she talking about?

Sierra sipped at her trendy iced coffee, wrinkling her nose. "What?"

Julia lifted the tote bag she'd come in with. "My manuscript. I brought it for you to review."

Grant narrowed his eyes at it as his mind worked to piece together the woman's reason for surprise. Had Sierra mentioned meeting with an author last night when she'd been babbling?

He held out a hand to slow the conversation and find more details, but Sierra was already reacting.

"I don't care about your manuscript," she said with a screwed-up face. "I want you to marry my dad."

Julia hesitated for a full breath, the shock on her delicate features obvious, though Grant wished he could hear her thoughts. His hopes tumbled as the woman's reaction bordered on incredulous. He'd seen this panicked, deer-in-headlights look before in his business dealings. He usually relished having his mark on the run, but this time he didn't.

"Wh-what?" Julia finally managed to spit out, her fingers tightened to a death grip on the table's edge.

They were losing her. If they didn't counteract this, she'd

never agree. Before Grant could step in, Sierra responded in typical Harrington shark fashion.

"Marry my dad." She grabbed the application and dangled it in front of the woman's face. "The interview you're here for."

Julia's eyebrows pinched, and her eyes darted from Grant to Sierra. "But I'm here for the publisher meeting about my manuscript."

Sierra's sharp features twisted with confusion. "What? What manuscript?"

Julia reached down and tugged a thick stack of papers from her tote bag, slapping it on the table and shoving it toward Sierra. "My manuscript. *The Illusion of Innocence.* You're my publisher."

Sierra's face went blank as she stared down at the black letters printed on the white paper. "Ohhhhh. You're *that* Julia Stanton. You were one of the authors with Heritage."

"Right," Julia said, with a nod.

"Uh, then why did you fill out this application?" Sierra pressed.

"I thought it was part of the interview process. You said all the authors were being reviewed."

Sierra's red lips formed a pout, and she narrowed her eyes. Grant recognized his daughter gearing up to go on the offensive. She'd made her choice, and she wouldn't let it go until she'd battered the competition into submission.

"Well–"

Grant grabbed her forearm and squeezed as he interjected himself into the conversation. "Obviously, there has been some sort of misunderstanding here. But–"

"But you still filled out the application. So, are you willing to do it or not?"

Sierra's statement stunned Julia into silence again. Her

eyes slid back and forth between the two of them as her lower lip bobbed up and down.

"Maybe if we–" Grant began.

"No," Julia burst, interrupting him.

Grant tugged his chiseled chin back toward his chest at the single word. He hadn't been told "No" very often, and the word still sometimes surprised him.

She flicked her gaze from him to the table in front of her, her features still stricken with surprise. "I-I'm sorry, I'm just here about the manuscript."

"To hell with the manuscript. We need you, not your book," Sierra shot back.

Grant lowered his voice to a hiss. "Sierra."

The pained expression on Julia's features could not be mistaken. She sat speechless for a moment before she grabbed the bound papers and shoved them into her bag.

"Wait," Grant said as she rose from her seat, muttering an, "okay."

He popped from his as she hurried toward the entrance. "Julia, wait!"

She wove through the remaining women in a flash, her hasty departure stirring the air. A blinding glare from the sun's reflection on the swinging door announced her disappearance from the club.

Grant flung his arms in the air, with a huff.

"Daddy! Do something!" Sierra demanded, with a stamp of her high heel on the floor.

Grant leaned over to grip the table, his jaw clenched. "What do you expect me to do? You've driven her away."

Sierra cocked her head. "If she can't handle what just happened, then she isn't the best candidate. She's going to have to deal with a lot more than that as the fifth Mrs. Harrington."

Grant slid his eyes closed before he shoved the table.

"See what I mean?" She arched an eyebrow at him as she straightened in her seat.

Grant pressed his lips together and sank into the seat Julia had just occupied. "I guess I'll call Mitchell. Maybe he–"

"He what?" Sierra asked. "Came up with another Hail Mary play overnight?"

Grant flicked his gaze under the table.

"Daddy?"

He leaned forward, hooked his finger around a worn leather strap, and tugged it upward. A purse dangled from his finger.

"She forgot her purse."

A smile tugged back one corner of his lips as an idea formed. This was the in he needed to turn this negotiation around.

"Big deal. I'll call a messenger to run it back to her. We have bigger problems to deal with." She snatched her phone from the table and tapped the screen.

Grant grabbed her wrist, stopping whatever communication she was sending. "No. I'll take it back to her."

Sierra rolled her eyes. "Seriously? This is a job for a courier. I'll pay extra to make it speedy."

Grant shook his head at her. "You're being short-sighted. You said yourself she was perfect."

"Ah, except she ran out of here like the roadrunner jetting away from Wile E. Coyote. She's not interested, which leaves us with one of the other ladies or scraping this entire idea."

"You have never been a subtle negotiator. You scared her."

"Like I said, she's going to have to toughen up if she's going to come into this lion's den."

"And she can. But we need her on board first. I can do that. With this." He lifted the purse in the air, with a grin.

"You're going to trade her purse for compliance?"

Grant's shoulders slumped at his daughter's hard-nosed

27

approach. "No, Sierra. I'm going to be a white knight and take this back to her, then convince her to take the deal."

He rose from the seat with the bag in hand as Sierra clicked her tongue. "Do you really think you can pull this off?"

Grant offered her a dimple-ridden smile and flick of his eyebrows. "Yes. I am, after all, Grant Harrington."

CHAPTER 4

JULIA

Still numb, Julia pushed out of the nightclub and into the fall air, grateful for the cool breeze that whisked past her as she navigated the crowded sidewalks. Overheated from the interaction, along with the misunderstanding, she shivered as the air slid through the tunic and hit her sweaty skin.

Horns blared as she darted around the corner, wandering through the city without a direction in mind. She weaved through the tangle of pedestrians, the city's pulse echoing her frantic thoughts. What had just happened?

Her mind searched to make sense of the odd interaction. She must have looked like a fool. And leave it to a billionaire to hold an audition for his latest wife.

Julia rolled her eyes as she shifted the weight of her manuscript on her shoulder and ran a hand through her hair. "I must have looked like an idiot."

Her mind replayed the details of the interaction over and

over, berating herself for the misunderstanding, and her reaction to it. She should have kept her cool and been more understanding. So many should haves. But she hadn't.

Shocked by the turn of events, she'd fled the interview after Sierra had told her she no longer cared about the manuscript.

She stopped on the corner, realizing she'd raced two blocks without even realizing how fast she'd been moving, or where she was going. Her hips told a different story, protesting the quick movements after so many hours in her barely cushioned chair.

As she sucked in a deep breath, the streets finally came into focus. At least she recognized them. She could find her way home at least, but she'd gone four blocks out of her way.

With no desire to go anywhere near the nightclub, she turned to cross the street. She ran straight into a fellow passerby and stumbled back a step. Annoyance crept through her, followed quickly by embarrassment again.

"I'm so sorry, sorry."

"Julia?" a familiar voice asked.

She raised her eyes to find a pert-looking blonde grinning at her. The woman looked vaguely familiar, but she couldn't place her.

"It's me, Bree. From the writing bootcamp."

Julia slid her eyes closed, recalling the woman's entry into their course's assignment: a cozy mystery about a set of talking pets who solved mysteries.

"Right, yes, Bree. I'm sorry, my head isn't with me today."

"Well, how are you?" Bree patted Julia's forearm, flashing her teeth again. "Don't tell me...you're great. How's your latest project coming?"

"Uhh, great," Julia answered with a fake smile, wondering how many shades of red she was turning from the lie. "Just talked to my publisher."

"Aw, that's so awesome. I'm officially published now, too."

Julia's grin wavered as Bree's success stabbed at her gut and highlighted her own stalled dreams. A pang of jealousy bubbled inside her, quickly turning to fear that perhaps she wasn't even the hero of her own story.

"Oh, really? With whom?"

"Myself." The outgoing lady thrust a fist in the air. "I opened my own little publisher. BreeZee Reads. Complete creative control over my work."

"Ah, how interesting. How have you found the experience?"

"Oh, so good," the blonde said, with wide eyes. "I've just had so many sales, it's incredible, and people are so supportive."

Julia forced a smile onto her face. Her failures shouldn't ruin this woman's successes. "Well, that's great. So good to hear." With her voice an octave too high, she hoped it sounded more sincere than it felt. As disappointed as she was, she couldn't rain on the bright light of Bree's enthusiasm.

Bree bobbed her head up and down. "We should catch up sometime. We can trade notes or maybe collaborate on something."

Julia forced a nod, her throat tight. "Definitely."

"I've got to run," Bree said, darting past her before she whipped around and held up her thumb and finger. "I'll call you!"

Julia waved with a tight-lipped grin as the woman waved and hurried away from her. She traveled another block out of her way before she made her loop back toward her place.

Her introverted nature drove her to seek solitude and solace by herself. She'd spent many a night consoling herself and licking her wounds. She could do it again.

She would find a new way forward. Her mind already

concocted query letters for new agents and publishing houses as a distraction from dwelling on the odd interaction.

Every so often, though, her memories flicked back to the strange experience. The flashbacks of the man's icy blue eyes on her made her feel mortified all over again.

Her steps became plodding as her can-do attitude deteriorated. She would have preferred to melt into the sidewalk than continue walking among her fellow citizens. It felt as though each one of them could detect her shame.

She couldn't get back to her apartment fast enough. The mortification made her quicken her steps, speeding through the streets until she arrived at her building.

Puffing for breath, she reached her floor, tugged open the metal door, and headed for her apartment.

She grabbed at her shoulder, freezing before she reached her door. No leather strap hung along with the tote bag. She glanced at her tunic, shoving her scarf aside. No purse.

Her stomach turned over. In her distracted flight home, had she dropped it? Or had someone swiped it while she waited to cross a street?

Her eyes slid closed, and she planted a palm firmly against her forehead. She hadn't picked it up when she'd absconded from the publisher meeting.

"I am so stupid."

She shifted her weight from one foot to the other as she vetted her options. Should she return for it, or was it possible for her just to leave it there and cancel her credit cards?

But it had her ID, along with her cards, phone, and keys. She needed it. She'd have to swallow her pride and return to the nightclub. If she was lucky, everyone would be gone, and she'd just have to pick it up from the bartender.

If the place was even open. When did nightclubs open? She hadn't been to one for quite a while. Probably late in the afternoon, if not in the early evening.

She pounded on her neighbor's door, hoping to find someone at home, but no one answered. Where could she go to wait until the nightclub reopened later today?

"Library," she murmured to herself.

She'd go do some research on paths forward until she could return to the nightclub for her bag. The elevator dinged, announcing someone arriving on her floor. With no desire to see anyone, she ducked back into the stairwell and descended to the ground floor, pushing back into the fresh air and heading for the library two blocks from her.

She darted through the quiet space, searching for a computer carrel in a remote corner. When she found one, she parked herself at the computer and searched for publishers. She found only a few accepting manuscripts. With an email to herself open, she typed in the names and pasted the websites of each one before sending it on its way.

Her mind spun out of control, darting in a thousand directions. To calm it, she opened another email and began to type, letting her pain and frustration flow out onto the page in the form of a new manuscript.

She clacked at the keys through lunch and into the late afternoon. Her stomach grumbled, but with no cash or credit cards, she ignored it until after four. She sent her work on its way to her inbox before she gathered her tote bag and left the computer station behind.

With a silent prayer that the nightclub would already be open, she navigated to it. Her heart fell as the giant letters remained dark. She approached the door and tugged on the handle. Locked.

With a hand pressed against the cold glass, she peered inside. Someone flitted past, with a case of alcohol. She rapped against the door and waved when they turned toward her.

"Help!" she called.

The muscular man offloaded his cargo onto the bar and hurried to the door. He flicked the lock and popped it open, sticking out his head. "We're closed."

"Yes, I know, I'm sorry. I was here earlier and left my purse. I wondered if I could just grab it from you."

He screwed up his face.

"My publisher, Sierra Harrington, was here doing interviews. I met with her and forgot my purse."

A flicker of pity crept over his features. "Oh, right, uh, I haven't seen it."

Her knees wobbled. "No one turned it in?"

"Nope."

She pressed her lips together as panic built. "Do you mind if I check the area where I left it?"

"Sure." He pushed the door open further, allowing her to duck inside. She hurried to the booth she'd sat in earlier, her cheeks burning with the memory of her earlier interaction here.

Upon a cursory glance, she spotted nothing. After climbing under the table and running a hand along the seat, she gave up.

"Find it?" The man glanced up at her from behind the bar as she passed by.

"No," she said with a shake of her head, trying not to sound so defeated. "Thanks, though."

"That stinks. I'll keep an eye out for it. Good luck. I hope you find it."

She nodded at him as she pushed through the door into the waning light of the late afternoon. Her steps quickened as she listed her next steps in her mind, each one a stepping stone back to some semblance of control.

She could go to a neighbor's and call the super. He could let her in. From there, she could call to cancel her cards and report her missing ID.

"What a fiasco," she murmured as she kicked a fallen leaf in front of her.

She reached her apartment building and climbed the stairs to her floor. As she pushed through the door into her hall, she froze.

A man leaned against the wall outside her door: Grant Harrington. His casual stance was a stark contrast to the turmoil of Julia's day.

He peeled himself up to stand and grinned at her. "You're a hard woman to get ahold of, Julia Stanton."

Julia tried to form words but found herself unable. What was he doing here?

She slid her eyes closed for a second before she took a step forward. Probably to berate her for running out on his daughter.

Before she could ask, he lifted his hand. Her purse swung from it. "Forget something?"

Her chest heaved with both embarrassment and relief. She couldn't decide if she wanted to rip it from his hands and disappear into her apartment or throw her arms around his neck.

"Oh, yes," she said, breathier than she would have liked. "Thank you. I went back to look for it. You didn't have to come all this way."

He smiled at her, dimples piercing his sculpted features. "Actually, I did."

She stared at him for a moment. She never could figure out what people meant by some of the things they said. Why did he have to return this to her?

"I think there was a big misunderstanding earlier, and I'd really like to discuss it with you, if you have a minute."

An uncomfortable feeling formed in the pit of her empty stomach. She really preferred not to, but the man had just brought her purse back, so she felt like a heel refusing him.

She swallowed hard and forced herself to nod her head. "Uh, sure."

She dug into her newly returned purse for her keys, unlocked her door, and pushed inside. She flicked on the lights, immediately regretting the move that called more attention to the austere apartment.

With a nervous grin, she slid a lock of hair behind her ear and dumped her things on her dining table-slash-workspace. "Can I offer you anything? Like..." Her mind searched her almost empty refrigerator. "Water?"

"No, thanks. Cute place."

"Thank you." She hated small talk. What was he doing here? She decided to cut to the chase and try to end the interaction. "Listen, I really appreciate you returning my bag, but there's no need to explain anything that happened earlier. I've been through the publishing process before; I understand how the business works."

He studied her for a moment, appearing to size her up. She shrank back a little under his scrutiny. Maybe she'd been too vocal. Maybe she shouldn't have said anything to him.

"I'm sure you have been, but this particular business has a plot twist you may not have been expecting."

She fluttered her eyelashes. Was it the lack of food making her dense, or was he talking nonsense?

"What do you mean?"

He studied her for a second before he let his gaze roam around her tiny place. "Let's just say there's a crucial plot point you're missing, and I think it may change things for you."

Julia struggled to glean the meaning in his vague statement, but perhaps all was not lost for her manuscript. Before either of them could speak, her stomach growled, splitting the silence. Julia pressed her lips together and shook her head.

"Sorry, I haven't eaten all day."

The statement seemed to please the billionaire. His lips curled into a smile. "Well, let me take you to dinner. We can talk there."

She stood stunned once again at the offer. Was this one of those times she was supposed to decline politely and let him go along on his merry way?

"Oh, no," she started, with a shake of her head.

"Come on, you're obviously hungry. Let me take you to dinner."

Her eyebrows pinched as she tried to come up with another way to decline politely when he held his hand out to her. "I'm not going to take no for an answer. And I promise you won't be disappointed."

She stared at him for another moment, a slight smile forming at the ridiculous situation. What was she about to get herself into if she accepted?

CHAPTER 5

GRANT

With practiced ease, Grant studied the woman in front of him. A rare sense of anticipation stirred. Something he hadn't experienced in years. But each glance and every tiny movement drew him closer to her, like a moth to a flame.

Had he been convincing enough to pique her interest? She assumed it all centered around her manuscript. Her supposition betrayed the importance the document played to her. He could use that to sweeten the deal.

"Shall we?" A hint of genuine curiosity colored his tone.

She'd declined once already. That was the second time he'd heard the word "No" from her. It was not a word he typically allowed in his vocabulary.

He detected a slight sag in her shoulders. The silent motion suggested involuntary surrender, a subtle cue he'd become adept at spotting.

"All right," she said. "Though, just returning the purse was really enough. I don't–"

"I promise, the returned purse was just the start of your story."

She pinched her eyebrows together at the vague line, and he flicked his eyebrows at her, pleased with his win. Soon, he'd have his next victory: this woman as his fiancee.

"My driver is waiting downstairs. Would you allow me the liberty of choosing a place I think you'll find...memorable?"

"Sure," she said, grabbing her purse and holding it up with a sweet yet disarming smile. "I'm not forgetting this again."

He led her into the hall. "Not unless you'd like to give me another excuse to rescue you."

A flush spread across her cheeks, and she averted her gaze, fiddling with her keys, a subtle surrender in their unspoken game.

It had been a long time since he'd made a woman blush. Most of the women who threw themselves at him were determined to prove they weren't shy.

"Okay, ready," she said as she shoved her keys into her purse and zipped it shut.

He offered his arm, pleased when she slid her delicate fingers around his bicep. He led her to the elevator and pressed the button. It seemed she was doing her best to look anywhere but at him, shifting her weight from side to side as they waited for the lift.

"I hope you didn't have to wait too long here," she finally said.

He offered her a genuine smile as the elevator doors whooshed open. "I would have waited as long as it took."

She offered him a fleeting smile that hinted at her confusion as they stepped inside the car and rode down to the lobby. During the short ride, he was acutely aware of every movement, from her tucking a stray lock of hair behind her ear to her shifting weight. As he led her from the building, his driver, James Bennett, tugged the back door of the Rolls and offered him a knowing smile.

"The Sapphire Room," Grant said as Julia climbed into the back.

A stiffness formed in Julia's posture as the name of the elite restaurant rolled off his tongue. A place of power plays and whispered deals, it provided an impressive location to make his offer.

"Right away, Mr. Harrington."

Grant slid into the seat next to Julia, and James slammed the door closed before hurrying around to his seat behind the wheel.

The buildings of New Orleans whisked past their window, lit by the energy his company provided. His thoughts drifted to the negotiation ahead. The weight of its importance settled on him like the jazz-filled air of the city.

Next to him, Julia licked her lips as she kept her eyes trained on the traffic they swerved through to reach the restaurant frequented by senators, CEOs, and sports stars.

James pulled up to the door and scurried from the car to open Grant's door. He stepped out, offering his hand to Julia. The soft touch of her fingers against his emboldened him as he helped her from the car and led her into the building's elevator. They climbed to the high-rise restaurant that towered above the city.

The black-clad hostess grinned widely at him as he led his date to her. "Mr. Harrington, so nice to see you back. We have your usual table waiting, if that's suitable."

"Yes, thank you."

She grabbed two menus and led them through the filled tables to a table near the window, framed with sapphire velvet curtains. Low-hanging chandeliers cast a warm glow over the room, and the dark walls absorbed the light chatter of its guests.

Grant seated Julia before swinging around the table to sit across from her. Their waiter already approached and greeted them.

Grant eyed Julia as she offered the man a kind smile, wriggling in her seat as she studied the menu with a tight-lipped expression.

"May I bring you something to drink?" the waiter asked.

"A bottle of your finest champagne. Perhaps a vintage Dom Perignon? We're celebrating a special occasion this evening."

"Very good, Mr. Harrington." The man scurried away to retrieve their drink when Julia flicked her gaze to Grant, her gaze questioning.

"Unless you don't think finding your purse is worthy of a celebration."

She offered him a breathy chuckle. "Their finest cham-pagne may be taking it a bit far for my thirty-dollar handbag."

"Well, I did promise more to come, didn't I?" He offered her a sly grin as the waiter returned with a bottle and show-cased it to him. After checking the year, he nodded, allowing the man to pop the cork and pour their glasses.

They placed their orders, and the waiter left them to enjoy their bubbly. As the man left, Grant raised his glass to Julia, the dim lights sparkling off the bubbling cider. "To an unforgettable evening."

He uttered the toast, oblivious to the shockwaves those four words would send through his life.

Julia raised her glass, a wavering smile crossing her perfectly formed lips before she took a sip and set the glass down against the crisp white linen. She toyed with the stem, tracing it up and down as she flicked her gaze to the window.

He eyed her while she admired the view as he considered his next move. "It's a beautiful view."

She offered him what he detected to be the first easy, genuine smile of the night. "Yes, it is."

He used the moment to lean closer to her. "Do you know why I picked the restaurant?"

She flicked her gaze back over the city laid at their feet. "I assume because you have a standing reservation for a table with a view."

He kept his focus trained on her as he gave his head a slight shake, a perfectly crafted and practiced move, even when uttering the truth. "The name reminded me of your eyes."

This time, there was no mistaking the color that flushed her face. She swallowed hard at the compliment, as though she wasn't used to receiving them.

The delivery of his steaming hot meal and her salad broke up the moment. Julia dove into her lobster salad, grateful for the distraction.

Grant paused, his fork hovering above the perfectly cooked filet mignon. "I owe you an explanation for this morning, but shall we enjoy our meal first?"

Julia glanced up from pushing the lettuce around on her plate. "Really, there's no need to explain. I understand the publishing company is heading in a new direction."

Grant tilted his head, his thoughts drifting, unbidden, to the empire he'd built from the ashes of his father's legacy. The thought of it slipping through his fingers after the many wars he'd waged filled him with a cold dread that contrasted sharply with the warmth of the room.

The tension in Julia's shoulders as they discussed her manuscript betrayed her concern over it in a physical manifestation. The small tell gave him enough to capitalize on it.

He leaned back slightly, giving her space, his voice soft-ening and eyes never leaving her face as he searched for any minute change in her expression to inform him of his next move. "I understand the importance of your work to you. And I want to support that."

She narrowed her eyes at him. "You brought me to The Sapphire Room to reassure me about my manuscript's acceptance?"

He polished off another piece of the tender meat and set aside his utensils, leaning closer to her. "No, not quite. My business with you revolves around the other part of the interview."

Julia paused, her muscles stiffening subtly, but enough for a practiced eye like Grant's to notice. "That was a mistake."

"I don't think it was." Grant held her gaze for a moment longer than most people were comfortable with.

Julia finally broke contact, letting her eyes slide back to the lobster on her plate. "I was there for my manuscript only. I'm sorry for the confusion, but I hadn't meant to apply for your contest."

"It wasn't a contest."

She flicked her gaze back to him.

He shook his head to add weight to the statement. "The thing is…I need your help."

The crinkle in Julia's brow betrayed her confusion, but the interruption of the waiter meant she'd have to wait for her answer. Grant couldn't have timed it better. The vague statement hung between them as the waiter inquired about dessert.

Julia politely declined, but Grant made certain they topped off their champagne glasses, the spark of hope still floating in his heart, like the bubbles in his glass.

As the waiter stepped away, Julia made her best attempt to put the conversation to bed. "Well, thank you for a lovely meal, Mr. Harrington–"

"Grant," he interrupted, leaning closer to her, "and that sounds like an evening-ending statement, but this evening is just beginning."

Her lips fell open as she searched for words. "I don't see how I can help you."

"Don't you?" He searched her face before he explained further.

"I don't see how."

He lifted his glass of champagne. "I'd love the opportunity to explain."

She gave him a slight nod, opening his way to make the offer.

"I'm not looking for the next Mrs. Harrington because I'm lonely. Sadly, the future of my business hinges on me changing my image a little. I'm sure you understand branding with your author business. I stand to lose everything if I can't change my image. The company I built will be ripped away from me."

"And you expect I can help...rebrand you?" she asked.

"I know it."

A soft laugh escaped her, tentative to start, as if she weighed the absurdity of the situation. Grant joined her in laughter, and her chuckle deepened, genuine amusement lighting her features.

"So, what do you say?" he asked when their laughter died down.

She flicked those blue eyes to meet his, the amusement still on her face. "I think you might be crazy."

He shook his head, still grinning at her. "No, definitely not. You're perfect."

He let the last word hang between them as she reddened again, allowing the conversation to lull as he searched for words. Silence stretched between them before he broke it, his urgent words tumbling from his lips in a desperate attempt to make her see the gravity of his need.

"Let me be completely honest with you, Julia, this is not a game. It's my entire life. Indulge me for a moment. When I took over Harrington Holdings as a young man, we owned a significant amount of assets, but nothing compared to the empire I built."

Julia's features settled into a neutral expression. She didn't understand or have any interest.

"I built Harrington Global piece by piece, painstakingly over the years. This isn't about corporate greed; it's about corporate pride. The business I slaved to build is being threatened. And along with me, the mismanagement I know will happen could cost thousands of others their livelihoods."

Her features softened as he continued his plea.

"Will you help me, Julia?"

Julia sat speechless for a few moments before she started to shake her head.

He grabbed her hand and squeezed. She froze as he spoke, plastering on a poker face that made her unreadable. "I'm being serious, and I have a very enticing offer if you'll agree to play the role of Mrs. Harrington. In return for you standing by my side, helping me re-establish my claim to the CEO role at Harrington Global for one year, I will pay you five million dollars."

Julia's eyes went wide, but a millisecond later he felt her hand begin to slide away from him. He was losing the battle. He needed a play, and quick.

"And I will guarantee your manuscript will be published."

She stopped, the newest addition to the deal sweet enough for her to consider, so he went in for the kill. He let his eyes rise to hers.

"Please, Julia, will you help me? Will you marry me?"

CHAPTER 6

JULIA

*A*n incessant pounding woke Julia from a dead-to-the-world sleep. She gasped, lifting her head from her pillow, her eyes slits against the bright morning sunshine.

She unraveled her body from the tangle of bedcovers and glanced at the clock. It was after nine. She hadn't slept this long in ages.

The pounding sounded again, echoing in her temples as she sat up. She rubbed at them as her heart slowed and disorientation subsided.

Before she could give anything any more thought, another knock came at her door.

"Coming!" she shouted as she dug for her robe amidst the comforter and tossed it around her shoulders. She flew out her bedroom door and to her front door, pressing her eye to the peephole.

A giant bouquet blocked most of her view. "Yes?" she called.

The man shifted the massive set of flowers sideways, revealing his courier logo stitched on his black shirt. "I have a delivery for Julia Stanton."

Julia ran a hand through her hair and scrubbed her teeth with her finger before she unlocked the door and pulled it open.

"Good morning," the man said, with a polite smile. He thrust a clipboard toward her. "Can you sign, please?"

"Sure," Julia said, accepting the paperwork and sliding the pen from the clip before she signed the highlighted mark.

The man skirted the door to set the large glass vase brimming with over a dozen long-stemmed red roses on her counter. She handed the paperwork back as he dashed for the door. She started to push it closed when he stopped her.

Her heart skipped a beat, wondering if this wasn't a flower delivery. The man grinned at her. "I've got more."

Her forehead crinkled as he carried in another set of roses. "More?"

"Plenty more," he answered as he retrieved another vase filled with roses.

Julia's eyebrows knitted as he carried vase after vase of red roses into her apartment, squeezing them into any space he could find.

"I'm sorry, this must be some mistake," she said after a few more vases.

"No mistake. I was told to deliver five hundred red roses to one Julia Stanton."

"Five hundred?" The overpowering scent of roses brought a rush of memories from the previous evening. Was this an apology or victory lap for Grant?

"Last one. Enjoy."

"Th-thanks," Julia stammered.

The courier stopped before he exited. Julia glanced around him, wondering if there was a mistake when she spotted another figure leaning against the door jamb. He held a bill between his fingers toward the man, who gladly accepted it.

"Thank you. You folks have a great day."

"Thank you," Grant said as he slipped into Julia's apartment, nonchalantly adjusting his cufflinks.

Julia's heart skipped a beat as her mind returned to the conversation the evening before. It had gone further into the night than she'd been prepared for. Grant had proposed. She'd said no. It was ridiculous, no matter what the reason was he'd given her.

But after a prolonged discussion, she'd finally said yes. She didn't know why she'd given in. Maybe she'd been tired, or maybe she'd seen the flicker of fear in his eyes and taken pity on him, or maybe she'd just done it so her manuscript would be published and she didn't have to go home, but either way, she'd said yes to him.

"What are you doing here?" Julia burst.

Grant's eyes twinkled as he studied her, still in her robe and pajamas. "Can't a man visit his fiancée?"

The rhetorical question stunned her into silence for a moment. She'd half-expected never to hear from Grant Harrington again after last night. Maybe what had happened had been some sort of game. Something bored people with money did for fun.

She had not expected him to show up at her doorstep with five hundred roses.

He moved closer to her, and she resisted the urge to back away a step. He reached into this pocket and withdrew a box. "Plus, I needed to drop off your ring. We can't have you showing up for your dress fitting today without your engagement ring, can we?"

"Dress fitting," she repeated.

The conversation rushed back in vivid detail. They were set to marry over the weekend. She had a dress fitting with Sierra that morning after they breakfasted together at Harrington House.

A dizzying rush of contradictory thoughts tumbled through her mind, turning her palms sweaty. In particular, she couldn't put her finger on why she'd agreed to this charade. In the cold light of day, it seemed like a terrible idea.

Grant laughed, his amusement seeming genuine. "You haven't forgotten your dress fitting, have you?"

She stared at him with a blank expression, and the smile slid off his face. "Have you?"

She shook her head, trying to compose herself. "No. Sorry, I just...thought I was meeting Sierra there."

His smile returned. "I thought it might be a nice surprise to drop by."

"Right," she said, her voice flat as a storm whirled inside her.

His confidence seemed to falter for a moment until she plastered on a tight-lipped smile. "And then there's the ring."

He waved the box in the air before he snapped it open.

Julia's eyes went round as she stared down at the massive diamond mounted on the white gold band. Its gleam nearly blinded her, cementing the reality of the commitment she struggled to grasp in the most ostentatious way.

"Please tell me that's not real."

"Of course it is," he said as he pulled it from the box. "Five carats, a bit on the small side, but your fingers are so delicate, I was reluctant to go bigger."

"Bigger?" she asked, her tone incredulous.

"Do you want a bigger one?"

"No. I don't even want this one."

Grant drew his chin back to his chest, obviously displeased by the statement.

Julia licked her lips, her shoulders slumping. Regret coursed through her as she wished she could reel the words back in.

"That's not what I meant. I just…I can't wear that."

"Why not?"

Julia finally tucked her eyes away from the massive rock and offered him an unimpressed stare. "I left my purse in a bar. Who knows where I'll leave your five-carat diamond ring."

He chuckled at her as he grabbed her hand. More memories of the evening before flitted through her mind as their skin touched. "Then I'll buy you another one."

"Besides," he added as he slid the ring onto her finger, "it's not *my* diamond ring you'll lose, it's yours."

She clicked her tongue at him as she struggled to come up with a response.

"Now, you'd better get dressed. Mr. Worthington does not like things to run off schedule. A fact you'll soon discover when you move into the manor." He offered her an amused grin.

"Mr. Worthington?" Her thumb rubbed the weighty ring around her finger.

"Our butler, darling. Oh, he'll likely want to speak with you about the schedule you'd prefer to keep." He waved a finger in the air as he nonchalantly passed along the last detail.

An overwhelming feeling made her knees wobble and stomach turn over. What had she gotten herself into when she'd agreed to be Mrs. Grant Harrington?

He reached for her elbow as he lowered his face to catch her gaze. "Are you okay?"

She focused on him as she forced a nod. "Yeah. Uh, just give me a minute to change."

"Take your time."

She dashed into the bedroom, kicking the door partially closed behind her. "I thought you said Mr. Worthington didn't want us to be late?" she called as she tore off her robe and tossed it on the bed before she rummaged through her drawers.

"He doesn't, but he works for us; not the other way around."

She raced to her closet and grabbed hold of a designer dress she'd splurged on last year. As she hurried toward the bathroom, she glanced through the ajar door, pausing for a moment as she spotted Grant reading the author quotes on her wall.

Somehow, the sight eased her frazzled nerves. With slightly less uneasiness, she stepped into the bathroom. After a quick brush of her teeth, she wriggled out of her pajamas and pulled on all the undergarments she needed before slipping into the dress.

After a quick brush of her hair, she pulled it into a ponytail and returned to her bedroom to pull on a pair of kitten heels.

She smoothed the dress down and took a second to steady her nerves before she emerged from her bedroom with her purse in hand.

He smiled at her as she emerged and offered his arm. "Ready?"

She answered with a nod, and within twenty minutes they were out of the city and heading down the gated, winding drive to the sprawling mansion past its manicured lawns at the massive fountain that wouldn't have fit in her apartment. She sucked in a soft gasp as she stared at the fairy tale landscape, wondering if her life there would be anything but.

Her heart rose into her throat as they approached the wide front doors under the portico. James hurried from the car to open her door before Grant's. She chewed her lower lip as she stared up at the house that would soon become her home, second-guessing everything.

Grant didn't allow her much time to dwell on it as he whisked her into the grand foyer. Her heels clicked across the bright marble floors. Her eyes went up to the enormous crystal chandelier hanging above them before Grant redirected her attention to the lithe man who awaited them inside.

"Worthington, right on schedule, I believe," Grant said.

The man bowed his head, topped with snow-colored hair cropped close to his head.

Grant waved to Julia. "Julia, this is our butler, Worthington. Mr. Worthington, my fiancée, Julia Stanton."

"So pleased to make your acquaintance, Ms. Stanton, and I look forward to serving your every need."

Julia offered him a wide grin, that overwhelming feeling again smacking her in the face. She didn't have much time to dwell on it. The clicking of heels drew her attention to one of the two sweeping staircases leading up to the second floor.

Sierra descended in a designer dress and pair of glittery heels that would give most women a nosebleed. She shook her head as she waved the morning's paper in the air.

"Have you seen this?" she asked, her voice tinged with amusement and satisfaction.

She hit the marble floor and paused, striking a pose against the railing as she flashed the article in question at them. "We could not have planned this better."

Julia studied the black-and-white photo, her eyes going

52

wide. The front page was dominated by a candid shot of her with Grant at The Sapphire Room, capturing her mid-laugh, eyes alight with genuine amusement, and Grant offering her an admiring stare.

The headline sensationalized the event. Grant squinted at the paper, reading the bold letters aloud. "City's most eligible bachelor off the market?"

A sharp laugh escaped Sierra as she spun the paper back to her, grinning at the article. "Oh, this is perfect. And the narrative writes itself–playboy falls for unsuspecting beauty. It's endearing, relatable. And most importantly, it's going to win the hearts of the public."

Grant poked a finger at his daughter. "Make sure the PR team sees this. We want to control the story, not the other way around."

Julia stared at the black flecks on the golden floor, wishing she could melt into them.

"Julia?" Grant's voice called, seeming far away.

She lifted her head, feeling the room spin. Grant's serendipitous grin melted into an expression of concern. "Why don't we sit down for breakfast?"

She nodded, hoping her legs would carry her to the chair. Grant led her through the house to a dining space with a table larger than she'd ever seen. "This is the casual dining space. We usually eat breakfast here, and most dinners."

Julia nodded as Grant pushed her chair in behind her. She tugged the napkin onto her lap. Mr. Worthington set a plate in front of her filled with a veggie omelet, crisp bacon, and two slices of buttered toast.

"Thank you," she whispered.

The man delivered plates to Sierra and Grant before he took a post in the corner of the room, ready to attend to any additional need.

Across from Julia, Sierra popped open a large folder. "All

right, I've got this going to press as an engagement party, during which you, Daddy, will announce that the two of you can't wait any longer and this will be your wedding." She poked a pen at him before continuing. "I've got most of the details taken care of as far as catering, cake, we're doing the dress today…"

She glanced up at Julia with a wrinkled nose. "It'll have to be off-the-rack, sorry."

"That's fine," Julia said as she tried to force some of the food down.

Sierra flicked up her eyebrows. "At least you're easy to please. I think the only other thing we need is your maid of honor."

Julia choked on the fresh-squeezed orange juice she sipped. "My what?"

"Maid of honor. I'm happy to step in and fill the role–"

"Sierra," Grant warned in a low tone.

"Daddy, I'm just trying to be supportive. But…" She shuffled her papers and poked a pen at one. "Maybe your sister, Alicia, would be available? That would look great."

"No," Julia answered quickly. She had no intention of telling her sister anything about this. Her mind flicked to the two missed calls she'd noted on her phone this morning. She'd have to find some way to explain where she'd been for the past twelve hours.

Both Harringtons set their questioning gazes on her. She hurried to explain. "Uh, she's not available. She's…busy."

Sierra studied her for a moment before she swiped a line across the page. "All right, she's out. Is there someone else?"

Julia offered her a blank stare.

Sierra leaned forward, an expectant expression on her made-up features. "Isn't there anyone you can call?"

Forty minutes later, they sat with mimosas in hand in the

Harrington House living room, with the bubbly Bree bouncing in the chair next to Julia.

"This is so exciting! Julia, you didn't even say anything yesterday when we ran into each other! Engaged! And your ring–to die for!"

Sierra downed her mimosa and waved the glass in the air for another. "We'll pick our wedding party dresses after Julia's picked her gown."

"I can't wait," the blonde cheered as a pair of black-clad ladies rolled in a rack of designer wedding dresses.

"All right, ladies, let's find a dress!" The pair whisked Julia away to begin trying on dresses. An endless parade of silk, sequins, and beads flowed as she stepped in and out of dress after dress after dress. From the bizarre to the extravagant, she and her small bridal party of two vetted through a multitude of dresses. They started to look the same to Julia after a while.

Exhausted, she was ready to draw a dress at random until they slid the last dress over her. With a subtle silver shimmer of beads, the shoulder-hugging dress fit her to her waist, where it flared into a sweeping gown.

Julia entered the living room, the fabric swishing around her, and glanced in the mirror.

"OMG, that dress is gorgeous! Oh, that's my pick. I love it!" Bree announced.

Julia let her fingers trace the silver beads as her mind drifted. Saying the dress was beautiful was an understatement. She'd imagined wearing one on her wedding day; she'd just never imagined her wedding day occurring like this.

"I do, too," Sierra answered in her understated tone, her perfect manicure tapping the champagne flute. "I'm not sure Julia's loving it, though."

Julia raised her gaze from the wedding-dress-clad woman

in the mirror, using the reflection to glance at Sierra. "No, I... it's beautiful."

She let her eyes slide back to her reflection, her voice turning dreamy. "It's elegant and classic. It's understated but fancy. It's..."

A tag poked her, and she glanced down at it, her eyes going wide and tone shooting an octave higher. "Thirty-five thousand dollars!"

Bree's lips formed an "O" as Sierra casually sipped her mimosa and joined Julia at the mirror. "So cheap. It's a shame we couldn't have gotten a one-of-a-kind, so this'll have to do."

"Sierra! This isn't cheap. This is someone's salary for a year."

Sierra furrowed her brow, a confused pout on her lips. "So, do you want another one?"

Julia pressed a palm against her forehead. It was too much. The mimosas, the dresses, the ring, the mansion. As she struggled to find an answer, a new voice entered the conversation.

"You look stunning in that."

"Daddy!" Sierra said, with a stomp of her heel. "You can't see her in this dress."

"That's an old wives' tale, honey," he said to his daughter as he strode across the room. "If this isn't the one, I can't wait to see what's better."

She brought her eyes to Grant's, her knees feeling weak. A subtle change in his expression betrayed some level of concern to her. He slid his arm from around Sierra's shoulders, setting his hand lightly on her forearm. "Ladies, would you excuse us for a moment?"

The staff from the bridal store shuffled from the room, along with Sierra and Bree, to peruse bridal party dresses.

Grant took a step closer to her. "Are you okay?

Julia tried to plaster a smile on her face, but she lacked the energy for it. "No."

"Why don't you sit down?"

She glanced down at the large dress around her legs. "I'm not sure I can."

He chuckled, though he sobered quickly when she didn't respond in kind. "Julia? Is everything all right?"

She hid her face with trembling hands as she shook her head before she glanced up at him. "I can't do this."

CHAPTER 7

GRANT

Grant minimized the spreadsheet he studied. The newsfeed on his browser scrolled with the latest stories from the New Orleans area.

The story about his supposed newfound love interest scrolled by on the carousel, flashing the picture of them at the restaurant. He clicked it and stared at the enlarged photo, focusing first on her face.

The beautiful smile, the laughter in her eyes. It was so removed from the poised women who sought to make a power play or land a rich husband.

His eyes shifted from her to his own face. His jaw clenched as he studied it. The candid moment betrayed emotion in his eyes he'd been careful not to let out for many years. He'd learned women preferred his money to him, so genuine feelings were something he couldn't afford.

With a stretch of his neck, he let his gaze go back to his fiancée. His mind went over her behavior from this morning as he drummed his fingers against the mahogany desk, as polished as his corporate facade. He'd noted her growing discomfort as Sierra had babbled about the wedding arrangements.

That she felt overwhelmed was obvious. With a deep breath, he turned off his screen, leaning back in his leather executive desk chair.

The double doors across the room swung open, and Worthington stepped inside. "Anything I can bring you, Mr. Harrington?"

Grant settled further into the supple leather with a sigh and shake of his head as he traced his lips with his index finger. He flicked his gaze to his butler, one of his closest confidants.

"How did Julia seem to you this morning?"

The man approached the desk, flicking his hands to the side before he clasped them together. "She seems like a lovely woman."

Grant eyed him. "That's not what I meant."

Worthington flicked his eyebrows in the air and bobbed his head up and down. "She seemed uneasy."

Grant poked a finger at him in agreement. "I had the same take. I think I'd better check on her."

"They'd had a steady supply of mimosas this morning, though it seems they haven't picked 'the one.'"

"I'm sure Sierra's been the biggest consumer of those," Grant said, his mind still searching the details of Julia's behavior earlier.

Worthington arched an eyebrow at him, reading his behavior easily after years of practice. "Is there something else, sir?"

"No," Grant said with a shake of his head as he rose and strode to the door, "but the last thing I need is a runaway bride."

"For the company's sake, or for your sake?" Worthington flicked his gaze to Grant, whose fingertips lingered on the door.

Grant gave him a knowing but unimpressed glance as he pushed through the door and into the foyer.

He strolled to the living room, where the dress selection still carried on. He wouldn't make an entrance; just ensure the process was going smoothly.

He glanced into the room, remaining behind the large ivory pillar holding the ceiling at bay. His lips parted as he sucked in a soft breath at the sight.

Julia stood in a stunning wedding dress, studying her own form in a full-length mirror. Something about her expression betrayed a depth to her.

Her bridal party approved, and he waited to hear her reaction. The corner of her lips tugged back as she listed the dress's virtues. Her last one, though, caused her alarm as she shouted the price in a shrill voice.

Sierra misunderstood her concern as a problem with the dress instead of its price—what she referred to as someone's salary for a year, and Julia spiraled further into her state of shock. He recognized the signs as she pressed a hand to her forehead, struggling to answer his daughter.

Should he do something? He answered his own question quickly.

He had to step in before this spiraled beyond his control and his plan went to ruin. He stepped from behind the pillar, approaching her.

"You look stunning in that."

Sierra protested his arrival with a stomp, but he fluffed her concern away, his focus on Julia. Something was wrong. Her facial expression reminded him of a deer caught in someone's headlights.

He touched her arm as he asked the others to give them a

few moments alone. They left the bride and groom alone, and Grant closed the distance between them.

"Are you okay?"

A faltering smile crossed her lips, but it faded quickly. "No."

Her creamy skin felt clammy to the touch and looked even paler than normal. "Why don't you sit down?"

Her eyes fell on the princess dress she wore. "I'm not sure I can."

The light moment of wit gave him hope, and he chuckled, but she didn't. The laughter quickly left him. "Julia? Is everything okay?"

Her hands shook as she covered her face, wagging her head back and forth before her glassy eyes met his. "I can't do this."

The four simple words punched him in the gut. He saw their perfect plan spiraling away, along with his company. He reacted quickly, leading her to the chair and easing her into it. The fabric splayed around her as she collapsed and started to apologize.

"Don't," he said, interrupting her before she could go any further.

She froze, stiffening as his sharp word sent her into a more guarded state.

"There's no need to apologize." He perched on the chair next to her.

She pressed her lips together and nodded. "Well, I hope–"

"Just a minute," he interrupted her again. "You're not off the hook yet."

She snapped her gaze to him, and he grinned at her in an attempt to defuse the tense situation. She started to shake her head when he stopped the gesture by holding up his hand.

"Julia, just take a breath."

She let her gaze fall to her lap, her chest heaving.

"I think today has been a little overwhelming, and I think that's understandable. But I still need you. That hasn't changed."

Julia glanced at him, her eyes pleading. "This is a terrible idea."

"It's not," he answered quickly. "We can do this. It'll get easier."

"Will it?" she questioned, her voice breaking. A shadow crossed her face, a flicker of something more than anxiety– regret, perhaps? Grant couldn't decipher it, but it lodged a worry deep inside him. He desperately sought to take control of the situation.

"Yes," he reassured her. "It'll settle down. But it's going to be overwhelming right now. Probably through the wedding. But after that…you can settle in here…focus on your writing. It'll be like a writing retreat."

She pressed her lips together, studying the intricate pattern of beads on her gown. Her eyes slid closed as though she was weighing something in her mind. Had he done enough to convince her to stay?

His usual ability to decipher what his opponent was thinking or feeling seemed less honed than usual. The high stakes must have been skewing his judgment. She slid her gaze to him, then away before she sucked in a breath and straightened.

"You're right," she said with a nod, flicking her gaze back to him. "I'm sorry."

A relieved smile crossed his face. "It's okay."

A soft chuckle escaped her. "I'm sure when you made your offer, you didn't expect your bride to be so temperamental."

Grant chuckled as he rose and helped her to her feet. "I've

dealt with many temperamental women in the past. Believe me, Julia, you are not one of them."

The crisis seemed to have passed. They only needed to ride out the next seventy-two hours until this plan came to fruition. Then the real work began. His mind had already begun strategizing his next moves with the board.

None of this mattered, though, if she didn't walk down that aisle and say her "I do"s. His mind returned to his butler's statement. Was it really the company he worried over?

He couldn't dwell on that now. The arrival of Sierra in a burgundy floor-length gown and Bree sporting a frilly deep purple ball gown ended his ruminating.

"I think that's more than enough time alone together. We have so many things to do yet, Daddy." Sierra grinned at her father as she paraded toward the mirror to study the dress.

Grant flicked his gaze back to his bride, trying to measure her current mood. "I'll see you for dinner?"

She offered him a slight smile and nod. "Yes."

The simple reassurance was enough to lift his mood. He kissed her cheek before leaving her behind with the others to sort out the details of dresses and colors.

"Aww," Bree gushed as he strode away. "He's so sweet."

He smiled at his own ability to charm most women, though a pang of fear coursed through him as he wondered if he could charm his own bride.

"Everything under control, sir?" Worthington asked as he strode across the foyer.

"Seems to be."

"The future Mrs. Harrington is happy?"

Grant paused as he mulled the question. Could he make her happy? He dismissed the idea as he faked a smile at the man.

"Everything's under control."

Worthington offered him a knowing smile, seeing right through his dodge. "Mitchell Caldwell is in your office."

"Right, thanks, Worthington." He clapped the man on the back as he strode toward his office.

He found his lead legal counsel sipping a glass of bourbon as he studied the painting of Grant's father over the fireplace. Grant swung the doors closed behind him before he crossed to the desk.

"Mitchell, do you have everything in order?"

The man twisted to face him. Grant recognized the look on his features. "Grant–"

"I don't want to hear it," he said as he sank into his chair. "This is the best plan we've got."

"Paying a woman to be your wife? If the board gets wind of–"

"They won't," Grant said, interrupting him. "And second of all, no money has changed hands."

"Yet."

"If we get divorced, it'll look like a payout in lieu of alimony. It's fine."

Mitchell narrowed his eyes at Grant. "Don't you mean 'when?'"

Grant slid his eyes closed at the misstep. "Right, when. Look, Mitch, this is not as bad of a plan as you may think. And wait until you meet her. I think you'll agree, we couldn't have done better if we tried."

Mitchell stalked to his open briefcase and pulled out a folded copy of the morning's newspaper. "She certainly has a wholesome enough look. I'd say any trouble will stem from people not believing a girl like this ever would have married you."

Grant chuckled at the statement as he flicked open the folder Mitchell handed him.

"Standard contract for services rendered. An early out

clause for you, if needed, and an out from payment if things do not go according to plan."

"In other words, if we don't maintain control of the company, she doesn't get paid."

"That's right. So, it's in her best interest to help you." Mitchell pressed his lips together and shrugged before he downed the last of his bourbon.

A flicker of doubt passed through Grant as he stared at the paperwork making their marriage nothing more than a job for her. He shoved it aside, closing the folder and sliding it to the edge of the desk.

"Perfect. I'll get Julia's signature on it at dinner."

"I'll keep it with the red files. This won't be filed anywhere else except with us. I wouldn't chance it."

"Of course."

"And then I'd start preparing the new missus for the barrage of questions she may receive from the board. You've got the Crescent City Charity Gala coming up just after the wedding. That'll be the first place people will pounce on her for answers."

Grant leaned back in his chair, the springs creaking, an echo of the tension in his mind. "I know."

"You're still planning on attending, aren't you?"

Grant considered it. Maybe it was wise to go alone or skip altogether, to give Julia more time to settle in.

"Grant, it would be a huge misstep to avoid it. Particularly after the wedding."

Grant flicked his gaze up to his lead counsel. "Maybe we'll be on a honeymoon."

The man's expression remained unflinching. "I would highly recommend you postpone your travels for the time being and attend to business here. You aren't marrying her for companionship; this is a business transaction."

The words jarred him more than he would have

preferred, but he nodded and rose from his seat, leading his attorney to the door. "Then we'll go. She'll be prepped and ready."

"She'd better be. I'm not going down for this ridiculous idea."

"Don't worry, Mitchell. I've got this all under control."

"I hope so." The man ducked out the door, heading for the front door to see himself out.

Grant heaved a sigh as he pushed the doors to his office closed and shuffled to the drink cart for a bourbon. He'd claimed he had it all under control. Did he? He'd forgotten about the gala. But Mitchell made an excellent point. It would be the best time for them to put in a public appearance as a newly married couple and cement in the board's minds that they were legitimate and solidify his new image.

Before he could dwell on it any further, a knock sounded.

"Yeah?" he called.

One door popped open, and Julia poked her head inside. "Worthington said you'd like to see me?"

"Oh, yes, come in. Would you like a drink?"

She eyed the bourbon in his hand before she shook her head. "No, thanks."

Was she nervous again? He licked his lips as he set his glass down on the desk.

"I have the contracts here to sign."

"Right," she said with a nod as he flicked the folder open and offered her a pen.

She accepted, biting into her lower lip as she stared down at the flagged space. The pen hovered over the paper, and for an instant he wondered if she wouldn't sign it. But a second later, she scrawled her name across the paper and handed the pen back, with a demure smile.

He scribbled his name on the second space and tossed the

pen on the desk before he flicked the folder closed. He stuck his hand out toward her.

"To a fruitful business partnership."

They shook on it before making their way to the dining room for dinner. Sierra babbled on about the remaining details of the quickly approaching wedding. Grant carefully eyed Julia's reactions, which remained neutral through most of the meal. She seemed content to let Sierra handle the details, a fact that may make this transition smoother.

After saying goodnight, she left, set to return the morning of the wedding. Grant settled into his office chair, kicking his feet up on the desk as he nursed a single malt whiskey.

Sierra sashayed through the doors and helped herself to a matching cocktail. She raised her glass to him as she eased into one of the chairs across from him.

"To winning this company back."

"Let's hope so."

She settled back into the chair, with an arched eyebrow. "Is there some concern it won't work out? It's been coming along without a hitch so far."

"So far. She hasn't said her vows yet."

"She will. She signed the contract, right?"

"She did."

"Then she has to go through with it. Or else she's in breach. If she gets out of line, I'll remind her of that."

"Sierra, go easy on her."

Sierra narrowed her eyes at him before she rolled them. "Oh, please, Daddy, just let this be a business deal, huh?"

Grant stared down into his drink. "It is. But we need her to play the role. Breach or not, if she walks out that door, it's over for us."

CHAPTER 8

JULIA

*T*he buzz of activity surrounded Julia as the stylist fussed with her hair, pulling it into a chic style fitting for her new role as Queen of New Orleans. That's what the papers said, anyway.

She bit back a cringe as she recalled reading the articles that had flooded the gossip columns for the last two days. The last two normal days of her life–or as close to normal as she'd get now.

Even they had been abuzz with preparations. Her apartment had looked fairly normal, despite the dozens of roses and empty closet that reminded her she'd soon no longer be living there.

And now the day had arrived.

Grant had sent James to pick her up early this morning. Guests had arrived at the house, and shortly after the party started, Grant had announced that this so-called engagement party would actually be their wedding, much to the guests' excitement.

A fluttering in Julia's stomach contradicted the calm she feigned. Her hands betrayed a slight tremble as she adjusted the pearls around her neck. She'd been whisked away by her bridal party to ready for the event shortly after the announcement, sparing her any awkward socializing.

She chewed her lower lip, awaiting the swish of lipstick to finish her perfect professional makeup.

In the corner, Sierra polished off another flute of champagne before she rose and shuffled forward in her high-heeled slippers. Still in a silk robe, but with finished hair and makeup, she awaited donning her red dress to lead off the bridal party's walk down the aisle.

In a last-minute development, Worthington had been chosen to walk Julia down the aisle.

Despite moving quickly, everything seemed slow, and she seemed to live outside of her body. Soon, the show would begin. Was she prepared for it?

The ceremony, the pictures, the first dance, the cake cutting.

The stylist misted a last spray of hairspray across her style, sending a mist of light floral scent exploding into the air. She stepped away as Sierra sidled up to her.

"I hope you're ready to smile. This pensive look just won't do for the pictures."

Julia raised her eyes to meet Sierra's through the mirror as she forced a smile onto her face while nodding.

"We need this to be convincing." Sierra narrowed her eyes, seeming to measure her up in the same practiced way her father gauged people.

Julia licked her lips, unsure of how to reassure her when she felt anything but sure about this arrangement.

Sierra smiled and patted her shoulders. "Just be yourself. You seem to have captivated the media."

"I'm not sure I did that, so much as my supposed relationship with your father."

Sierra gave her a stern look and wagged her finger. "Now, now, let's not use the word 'supposed.' Your relationship with my father."

"Right," Julia said, with a nod.

The conversation closed as Bree burst into the room in her breezy, one-shoulder maid-of-honor gown. Unable to contain her excitement, she struggled to slide her dangling red earrings into her ear with her shaky hands.

"My turn!" Sierra flitted into the en-suite bathroom of what would become Julia's suite when she moved into the mansion.

Bree finally finished with her jewelry and hurried to Julia's side, doing an excellent job of playing the attentive maid-of-honor. "You look beautiful. Do you need anything? Maybe another glass of champagne?"

"No, thanks. I'm just ready to get the dress on."

She squealed with excitement. "It's so exciting. Come on, I'll help you."

Julia rose from her seat as Bree uncovered the princess-style wedding gown and removed it from its hanger. Julia stepped into it, feeling the weight of the garment the moment she slid into the arms. It cemented the reality of the gravity of the situation she entered.

"Oh my gosh, you must be so excited." Bree offered her a wrinkled-nose smile as she started to fasten the dress. "He's so sweet, and super handsome."

"And so very in love with Julia," Sierra announced as she sashayed across the room in the designer dress.

"That's obvious," Bree said, with a nod. "Gosh, I hope I'm as lucky as you."

Julia held back a scoff. Maybe this would be easier to pull off than she expected. Bree was fooled. Would everyone else be?

They finished readying her, settling the veil in her chignon and fluffing. Tears shone in Bree's eyes as she pressed her hands to her cheeks. "Ohhh, you just look stunning. Oh, gosh, I always cry at weddings. I'm sorry."

Julia spun to pull the woman into a hug. She held onto her, allowing Bree to ground her.

"Ready?" Sierra asked, breaking up the moment.

"Uh, can I just have a moment?" Julia asked.

Sierra arched an eyebrow, her lips puckering. "Don't be too long. Our guests are getting hungry."

Julia offered her a fleeting smile and nod. Bree grinned at her as she grabbed her bouquet and headed out of the room. Sierra lingered in the doorway with a last glance before she finally disappeared into the hall.

Julia finally let out a breath. She swallowed hard, trying to dislodge the lump forming. She twisted to face the mirror, studying her countenance. Her mind regressed to someone else. The man she'd originally pictured donning a wedding dress for once.

She never expected her wedding day to be like this one, but maybe that was for the best. She lifted her chin. Maybe a loveless marriage was the best kind.

"He's going to be very happy when he sees you in that dress," Worthington's voice said from behind her.

She spun to face him. "Mr. Worthington," she said, her voice catching with surprise.

He smiled at her, offering her a fatherly gaze. "Are you ready?"

She plastered on a smile, trying to summon the courage to say yes.

He crossed to her, giving her a tight-lipped grin. "I know the arrangement. You'll be fine."

She blew out another sigh, tears threatening from the sheer emotion of the day. "I'm glad you think so."

His smile broadened. "Mr. Harrington chose very well."

The man's calm demeanor was the steadying force she needed to settle her nerves. This time when she smiled, it was genuine.

"Now, let's go finish this so you can begin to settle in. We look very forward to having you among the household." He offered his arm, and Julia accepted.

Music floated up the curved staircase as Worthington led her down it. They arrived at the ballroom, the din of guests escaping through the closed doors.

Julia's heart pounded as the music changed and doors opened. Sierra plastered a smile on her face, raised her chin, and strutted into the ballroom.

On the next round, Bree disappeared from sight, and Worthington led Julia to their spot on the carpet. She blew out a shaky breath.

"Just put one foot in front of the other," Worthington said to her as the door *whooshed* open.

Camera bulbs flashed as Julia offered him an appreciative smile. She glanced down the aisle, her mind replacing her soon-to-be spouse with another for a millisecond before Worthington led her down the aisle on rubbery legs as they passed the excited grins of the guests. With a shake of hands, Worthington handed her to Grant.

"You look stunning," Grant whispered as they stood in front of the officiant.

Julia smiled at him, heat creeping across her cheeks, her mind reminding her that this was his fifth wedding. He was a seasoned pro and had probably whispered the same thing to every woman he'd been in this position with. She searched his face for any indication of the lie, but his practiced countenance betrayed nothing.

Julia's mind blurred as the man launched into the wedding ceremony. His deep voice announced the reason for their gathering. The lump in her throat grew as he read off the commitments they were agreeing to. Ironic that the promises she would agree to in minutes were governed by a simple contract.

She managed to choke out her "I do," though his seemed to flow off his tongue easily.

She desperately tried to steady her trembling hand as they exchanged rings. Grant slid hers onto his finger easily, though the weight of the new item felt oddly heavy.

Within minutes, they were pronounced man and wife.

"You may now kiss the bride," the officiant said.

Julia offered Grant an awkward smile. He leaned closer to her, and she expected a quick peck before they paraded down the aisle. Instead, he cupped her face gently in his hands and pulled her in for a kiss that couldn't have looked fake to any onlooker.

The guests applauded as he pulled away and offered his arm to lead her down the aisle to the awaiting reception.

As the guests gathered for appetizers, Julia found herself ushered onto the manicured lawn for pictures. Sierra shoved a champagne flute into her hand, and she downed half of it before plastering on a smile as the photographer began snapping shots.

"Okay, just the maid of honor and the best man." A few people stepped away from the posed picture before flashbulbs blinded her again.

"And now, stepdaughter with new stepmom."

Grant stepped away, and Sierra took his spot. She wrapped her arm around Julia as she grinned. "You're killing it. People love you."

She let her face rest as Grant and Sierra posed together before they pulled her in for intimate photos of the bride and groom.

"Perfect," the photographer said as she snapped shots of Julia with her hand placed perfectly on Grant's lapel, her stunning engagement ring sparkling in the afternoon sun.

"And now, how about a kiss?"

Grant cupped her face again, his light eyes sparkling playfully. "Pretend I'm your favorite book–impossible to pull away from."

She burst into a laugh, a moment of genuine levity amidst the social pressures.

The camera clicked several times as the photographer crooned, "Ohh, that's perfect."

They finished with the photos, including the awkward kiss, before they entered the reception. It all became a blur as face after face offered her their best wishes and congratulated Grant.

Exhaustion coursed through her when the last guests finally left. She climbed the stairs to her suite, collapsing in the soft armchair, and kicked off her shoes. The dress swished around her as she fell back against the cushioned back. Her muscles ached from the tension she'd held in her body through the hours-long event.

She slid her eyes closed, promising herself a full day of writing the next day, to escape from the pressures of today.

A quiet knock sounded at the door. She found the strength to force her eyes open, spotting Grant, his bowtie undone and dangling around his neck.

He held two tumblers in his hands. "How are you holding up?"

She sucked in a breath as he strode toward her, offering him a weak smile. "I'm okay."

"You did well today. Everyone loved you." He clinked his glass off hers before he raised his in the air.

She stared down into the amber liquid as her fingernails tapped the glass. "It seems to be coming together for you."

"For us," he said, with a tilt of his glass. "We're partners in this, remember?"

She shifted back in her seat. "Right."

"Speaking of, we have the gala Wednesday night. There will be plenty of board members there for us to impress."

"I'll be ready," she answered, not certain she would be.

"Good." He studied her over the rim of his glass.

"I promise, I won't fall apart again."

"I wasn't thinking that." He paused for a moment before he polished off his drink and rose from his chair. He kissed her on the cheek. "You did well today. We've got this in the bag. See you in the morning."

He left her behind, pulling the doors closed. She managed to wriggle out of her dress and into her cozy pajamas, feeling more like herself the moment the soft flannel touched her skin.

She crawled into bed, finding herself unable to sleep, despite her exhaustion. The new room set her on edge. The bed felt strange, the lights were in different places; nothing was familiar.

She gave up after an hour and climbed from the high bed to retrieve her laptop. Disappearing into her latest manuscript, she allowed the familiarity of the work and her words to surround her in comfort.

When she awoke early the next morning, the laptop's blank screen stared back at her. She slammed the top closed before she crept from her bed, changed clothes, and snuck downstairs to make herself a quick breakfast before the staff rose.

She polished it off and hurried from the house, seeking fresh air and alone time to center herself. Her feet hit the pavement with no direction in mind, but she found herself strolling down the driveway toward the road. Her heart pounded suddenly, quickening her pace and increasing her panic.

The manicured lawns pressed in around her, still and quiet at this early hour. It seemed oppressive, driving her to reach the road faster.

She escaped through the wrought iron gate, glancing back through it at the sprawling mansion. In the night, it looked more staggering than during the day.

Julia reached into her pocket and pulled out her phone. Her hand lingered over one contact before her thumb finally pressed the call button.

A tired voice answered on the other end.

Julia twisted away from the house, a hiccup in her voice. "Alicia, I think I messed up."

CHAPTER 9

GRANT

Grant straightened the knot on his tie before he pulled his jacket on and smoothed the lapels.

"Is Julia up yet?"

Worthington brushed Grant's shoulders before replacing the brush on the valet. "Yes."

"That sounds cryptic." Grant raised an eyebrow at him through the mirror as he fiddled with his cufflink. "How is she this morning?"

"I don't know. I haven't seen her."

Grant whipped around to face his butler. "What do you mean you haven't seen her?"

"I mean just that, sir. She arose before any of the staff, made herself breakfast, and left the estate."

Grant's heart skipped a beat. "She left? To go where? Who took her?"

"She left on foot. The security footage shows her slip

through the gate at the end of the driveway before making a phone call."

"What time was this?"

"Around four forty-two."

He cursed under his breath as his mind stretched to damage control for the possible scenarios. An unexpected twinge twisted in his chest as an unfamiliar blend of concern and something else he couldn't pinpoint gnawed at him.

"All right. Call the security team. Check her apartment, the friend's place...what was her name? Bree? Check everywhere. Find her."

Worthington nodded before he spun on a heel to leave the room. Grant rubbed his chin as he processed the news and subsequent fallout. His new bride leaving him the day after their wedding would not bode well. In fact, it would worsen his image. He couldn't afford this. He had to find Julia.

He strode from the room, determined to comb the city for her, alongside his trusted butler.

"Good morning, Daddy," Sierra cooed as he approached the stairs.

"Not at the moment, it's not." He brushed past her, his features set as he hurried down the stairs.

"What's that supposed to mean?" Sierra hurried to follow him, her smile fading into a pinched expression. "What happened?"

"Julia's gone." The words stuck in his throat more than he expected.

"What?" The shrillness of her voice betrayed her shock. She froze on the stairs as he continued to the bottom before she hurried down them as fast as her five-inch heels allowed. "Where did she go?"

"No one knows." He stopped to face his daughter,

running a hand through his hair before he huffed. "She left before five this morning. She called someone."

"Can the security team track her phone or her calls?"

He pushed himself to move into the austere elegance of his office. Each step echoed off the polished mahogany floor as he entered the sanctuary of control and order, but today it felt like a stage where an unscripted drama was about to play out. He needed to move to feel in control of the situation that spiraled beyond his grasp.

"I've already asked Worthington to call them. We have to find her."

Sierra hurried behind him. "No kidding. Especially before she does something stupid."

Grant hesitated as he stepped behind his desk.

Sierra filled in the gaps as she paraded back and forth in front of his desk. "You don't think she went to the press, do you? Maybe an early morning call to a reporter?"

Grant's jaw tightened, his silence a fortress guarding his deepest fears. He'd learned over the years playing it close to the vest was often the best move until more information presented itself.

Worthington rescued him from comment a moment later, with Maxwell Sterling, the head of his security team, trailing behind him. The man adjusted the button on his dark suit, swiping a hand through his closely cropped hair.

"Max, tell me we at least know which direction she went when she left the property," Grant said, his hands on his hips.

"She went east on foot."

Sierra scoffed at the response. "That means zero. Which way did she go? Toward the city, or away from it?"

"Away," he answered.

Grant cursed under his breath. A tangle of worry and annoyance competed for his attention. Her disappearance alarmed him, but it also came with the worry of what damage this could do to the meticulously crafted image they were trying to portray.

She wasn't heading to her apartment or any place in town that would be easy to find. She could be anywhere. She could have gotten into a car with someone and be out of the state by now.

"What about the phone call?"

"We're reviewing the security footage now and trying to determine who she may have been calling."

"Can't you trace it? Can you track her phone?" Sierra asked.

Max flicked a sheepish gaze from Sierra to Grant. "We... don't have Mrs. Harrington's number."

Grant slid his eyes closed as frustration raised his blood pressure and made his tie feel too tight around his neck.

"If you pass it along to us, we can start tracking her right away."

"I don't have it," he said through clenched teeth.

The discreet security agent let his eyes slide to the thick burgundy area rug under their feet, careful to let the glimmer of disappointment not show through, though to Grant's trained eye, it did.

Grant gripped the edge of the desk, his knuckles whitening. "I don't even have my own wife's cell phone number. That's wonderful."

"How did you contact her?" Max asked.

"I...went to her place. I never called her or texted her."

All eyes turned to Sierra. The woman screwed up her face and shrugged. "I never called her."

"How did you handle the wedding arrangements?" Worthington asked.

"Email or direct message through social media. I never called her."

Grant snapped his fingers as his mind worked to resolve the problem. "What about her application?"

"You mean...from the thing?" Sierra asked.

"Yes," Grant snapped, his voice sharp with urgency, "you asked for contact information, didn't you?"

Sierra shifted an uncomfortable gaze to her father as she wrapped her arms around herself. "I burned all of it. Evidence, you know?"

Grant collapsed into the chair. "So, we have no idea what her number is. No one here has a clue as to what my wife's cell phone number is. Well, that's simply perfect."

"We can try to track it down. It may take some time–"

"Time we don't have. Get someone on the road in the direction she went. See if you can find her."

"Already done, sir, and we will continue to work the cell phone angle. I'll report back as soon as I have any information."

Grant swiped at the pencil cup on his desk, sending it flying across the room as he cursed again. The scattered pens clattered across the floor, echoing the chaos in his mind.

"That solves nothing, sir," Worthington said. "Perhaps some coffee, and maybe some breakfast."

"I can't eat."

Sierra exchanged a glance with Worthington, her concern apparent. "Daddy, you really should eat something."

"Don't patronize me, Sierra."

"Coffee," she mouthed to Worthington, who nodded and disappeared through the double doors to retrieve the beverage.

"Where could she have gone?"

Grant's mind wandered briefly to the moment they'd shared yesterday before their kiss for the camera. They'd shared a laugh. That laugh, genuine and unguarded, stuck in his mind, a stark reminder of the woman beyond the contract. Had he gotten this bad at reading people that he didn't see the warning signs?

He sank his chin into his palm as he stared at the sparsely decorated desk. He'd planned to put a wedding picture right next to the lamp. A photo may be all he had left of the woman.

Worthington arrived with coffee for both Grant and Sierra, along with breakfast plates, shuttled in by a maid. Grant sipped at the dark liquid before he shoved his untouched plate aside, his stomach knotting.

The phone on his desk rang, the jarring sound startling him. He snatched up the receiver and growled into it. "Tell me you have something."

"Nothing yet, sir," Max's voice answered. "We did a sweep of her apartment; she isn't there. A drive-by of Bree Montgomery's place didn't turn anything up."

Grant heaved a sigh at the unwelcome news. "Then keep looking."

He glanced at his watch, the diamonds on the face sparkling even in the dim light. "It's after seven. She has been gone for over two hours. Do you know how far she could have gotten by now?"

"I understand, sir. We're doing our best to track her with every resource. I'll keep you informed."

"Find her," he barked before he slammed the receiver onto its base.

Sierra froze in mid-chew of the strawberry she'd popped into her mouth, shifting it around before she spoke. "Maybe you should try more coffee, Daddy."

He glared up at her as she shrugged, no stranger to the scrutiny of Grant Harrington.

"You seem stressed."

"Is there a reason I shouldn't be? My new wife is missing."

She knitted her brows as she waved her phone in the area.

"Right, but there's no reason to panic yet. A quick scroll through my newsfeed doesn't show anything untoward. So, if she's talking to the press, they haven't run with the story yet."

He bit his tongue. Sierra's only concern was PR, and she assumed his was, too. Yet the knot of tension between his shoulder blades was not due entirely to the image management crisis he faced.

Another hour passed, with no news. The food, now cold and unappealing, still sat untouched as Grant drummed his fingers on the mahogany desk.

Sierra paced back and forth in front of the fireplace scrolling through her phone. Her expression tightened.

Grant eyed her. "What are you looking for?"

"Just making sure Julia hasn't...you know...outed all of this on social media."

"Not everyone posts every minute of their day on their socials, Sierra."

"Obviously." She scoffed. "The last post she made was, like, months ago. Who goes that long without posting something? Anything?! We really need to do something about updating this when she's back."

When.

The word rattled through his mind, and he tried to take solace in Sierra's obvious belief that Julia would return.

His phone rang, and he snatched it. "Anything?"

"We had a sighting at a nearby park," Max said in his ear. "We're tracking it now. I'll patch in the live feed."

Grant's fingers tightened around the phone, hopeful.

"Approaching her now," a man's breathy voice said. "Excuse me, ma'am? Ma'am? My apologies." There was a brief pause. "False alarm, it's not her."

Grant slammed the receiver down as the clock on the mantle chimed eight. He leapt from his seat.

"Where are you going?" Sierra demanded.

"Out to find her. I can't sit here anymore."

He burst through the doors of his office into the foyer, stopping dead as he stepped onto the marble floor. Sierra plowed into the back of him, clicking her tongue at him.

It didn't matter to him. The corners of his lips turned up at the edges as he watched the brunette casually slick a lock of hair behind her ear as she pushed the front door closed.

"Julia."

She snapped her blue-eyed gaze to him, offering a fleeting smile. "Good morning."

He crossed to her, clasping her shoulders. "Where have you been?"

She offered him a confused glance, sliding her gaze to the door. "I needed some air. I went for a walk."

"At quarter to five in the morning?" Sierra asked over his shoulder. "For hours?"

Julia knitted her brows. "Uh…"

Grant stepped in to defuse the situation before it devolved into another crisis he didn't need. "We were worried about you."

"Worried?" she repeated, her voice soft.

Sierra waved a hand in the air. "Uhhh, yeah. Hello? You left before five in the morning, made a cryptic phone call, and disappeared for hours the day after your wedding."

Julia's features pinched as she focused on Grant, searching his features as she laid a gentle hand on his forearm.

"Ah, Mrs. Harrington, I see you've returned and all is well," Worthington said as he entered the foyer and crossed to them, clasping his hands in front of him. "I will call off the dogs."

Julia knitted her brows, flicking her gaze from Worthington to Grant. He opened his mouth to respond when Max hurried in. "I've started to track her–Mrs. Harrington, you're back."

She arched an eyebrow before setting her surprised gaze on Grant. "I hadn't realized my morning walk would cause an international incident."

Grant chuckled at the joke as he wrapped his arm around her. "Like I said, we were worried. And then we realized none of us had your phone number, so we couldn't call you. Why don't we rectify that now?"

"S-sure," she stammered as Grant slipped his phone from his breast pocket and readied it for her number.

Sierra tapped it into her own device with narrowed eyes as Julia rattled off the number.

Grant grinned at her as he slid his phone back into his pocket and held out his hand. She stared down at it, her confusion still not cleared up.

"Well, I should give you my number. It would make sense for you to have your husband's number saved in your phone."

"Right," Julia said as she fished it from her pocket and handed it to him.

Before he could return it, Sierra snatched it with a broad smile. "And of course your stepdaughter's number."

She typed in her information before she handed it back, with a smile. "Here you go."

Julia offered her a tight-lipped smile before a tense silence enveloped the group. Grant broke it first.

"I should head into the office."

"Yes, you have a corporation to win back," Sierra said, with a pump of her fist.

Grant eyed his new bride. "Perhaps you could join me for lunch?"

She hesitated, a fact that did not escape him. "Uh, sure."

"Excellent. I'll see you around one? Just have James drive you."

She smiled and nodded before she left the scene behind, scurrying up the stairs. Grant followed her flight, his mind still swimming with questions he may never have answers to.

"Well, well, well," Sierra said, "what do you think the real story is?"

"She's back. That's what matters." Grant adjusted his cufflink before he checked his watch.

"She called her sister."

"What?" he asked.

"The phone call she made was to Alicia, her sister. I checked her call log when I put my number in."

"Sierra, I think it's best if we let this go. She went for a walk. We now know how to contact her, so if this happens again, we can very quickly track her down instead of panicking."

He strode to the front door, prepared to head to the office as Sierra twisted to Max. "Keep a tracker on her phone, just in case."

He slid his eyes closed as he stepped into the now-bright morning sunshine. It would be a miracle if his new wife survived her new lifestyle. She'd likely rue the day she ever set foot in that nightclub.

James opened the door for him.

"Sorry for the delay, James. We had a minor crisis this morning."

James climbed behind the wheel, flicking his gaze into the rearview mirror. "I heard. Everything okay now?"

"Yes, Julia came home a few minutes ago. She seems fine. Just a morning walk. Apparently, she's an early riser."

"Very early, from what I hear," James said.

"Yes." Grant's lips tugged up at the corners as he recalled the moment she'd walked back through the door. "Crisis averted. Oh, and Julia will be joining me for lunch. Can you bring her to the office around one?"

"Absolutely, sir. Do you need me to make a reservation anywhere?"

"I'm thinking the Garden Terrace."

"She'll love that," James said as the city's buildings closed in around them. "I'll make sure you have a view of the water."

"Thank you. I'm sure she'll love that."

They arrived at the Harrington Global offices. Grant adjusted his tie as he rode up to the top floor in the elevator. A bevy of good mornings met him as the doors swung open. He met them with grins and nods as he wound back to his office.

The fine lines around his secretary's eyes crinkled more as she smiled at him when he entered and popped from her desk with the enthusiasm of a twenty-year-old, despite being over a decade older than him.

"Good morning, Evie."

"Good morning, Mr. Harrington. How was your weekend?"

"Excellent," he said as he slid his briefcase across the desk's top and took his place behind it. "It was a very productive weekend, and I'm ready to tackle the issues facing us."

Evelyn shifted the folders pressed close to her conservative navy blazer. "Those are many, sir. I'm sorry to be the bearer of bad news, but the hits just keep coming."

She dumped the folders on his desk. "I've sorted them by order of most pressing to least, though the least pressing is two suppliers pulling out of potential contracts, so that'll give you an idea of how bad the top folder is."

Grant's enthusiasm for the day suddenly waned, though tackling corporate problems may be just what he needed. A welcome distraction from the personal matters that had taken over his life as he tried to save this company.

"I'm not sure I can thank you for dumping these problems on my desk, but I appreciate your work on these."

Evelyn tucked a lock of her gray hair behind her ear, with a smile. "If you need anything, just let me know."

"You know I will." Grant collapsed into his chair and dove into the first file.

Two hours and dozens of calls later, he hadn't made headway on one of the dozen folders Evelyn had dumped on his desk.

He blew out a sigh as he leaned back in his chair and looked over the city outside his window. If he wasn't able to solve some of these problems soon, his image may be the least of his concerns. What he couldn't understand was why he was suddenly losing ground on all fronts.

A buzz interrupted his thoughts. He swiveled his chair around to answer his secretary's call.

"Yeah?"

"I'm sorry to interrupt, Mr. Harrington, but you may have another problem to add to your list."

Grant twisted to stare out the window again, the weight of his corporate world crashing down on his shoulders. "One crisis to the next," he muttered.

CHAPTER 10

JULIA

*J*ulia blew out a heavy breath as she eased into the desk chair. A part of her new suite, the writing office overlooked the back gardens at Harrington House. The soft morning light filtered through the window, casting a warm glow over the antique desk. The furniture had been carefully laid out to maximize the view, though she wasn't certain if it would be an inspiration or a distraction.

The serene beauty of the gardens outside, with its brilliant fall colors, contrasted starkly with the tightness knotting the muscles across her shoulders, a tangible sign of her inner turmoil.

She let her chin fall into her palm as she drummed her fingers on the top of her laptop. Her morning had started off oddly. She reflected on the conversation that had just occurred in the foyer. The expression on Grant's face, the tightening of those fine lines around his eyes, had been odd.

It almost showed genuine concern for her whereabouts. An emotion she couldn't identify fluttered in her stomach. Was she pleased about that, or did it set her further on edge?

She flicked open the laptop. He likely had polished his concerned face many years ago for press conferences.

She shoved her musings aside to focus on her manuscript.

"Working on that next book?" Sierra's voice asked from her doorway.

Julia swiveled around in the high-backed chair to eye her at the door leading to the hall. "Uh, I hope so."

"I bet you do."

Julia's smile faltered as she tried to make sense of the quasi-threatening words. Sierra sauntered further into the office, running a manicured nail over the well-polished workspace table tucked near the doorway.

She picked up one of Julia's reference manuals and thumbed through it before she set her gaze on Julia.

"Is there something I can help you with, Sierra?" Julia asked after a tense moment.

A Cheshire Cat grin curled Sierra's ultra-red lips. "I am so glad you asked. Would you mind sharing with me what prompted you to flee Harrington House before five, call someone, and then not return for hours?"

"I told you, I was taking a walk."

"A three-hour walk?" Sierra questioned. "Really?"

"I walk a lot when I'm thinking through plots. Sometimes for hours."

Sierra arched an eyebrow. "And the phone call."

Julia frowned, pondering her response. She didn't feel she needed to explain her personal calls to her new stepdaughter. Then again, the worry she'd seen etched in Grant's face earlier made it clear they were concerned.

"Personal," she decided. "Nothing to do with what we're trying to achieve here."

"Personal? I do hope my new step-mommy isn't harboring a secret that may catch the media's attention."

"Of course not."

Sierra narrowed her eyes, sizing her up. Julia stood her ground, raising her chin and holding her gaze.

"All right. That's good enough...for now. Just...next time think ahead, huh? Grant Harrington's new bride decides to take a three-hour walk in the wee hours of the morning mere hours after the wedding just doesn't look right."

Julia swallowed hard. No wonder Grant had looked so worried. The PR nightmare that may have unfolded wouldn't have been easy to manage.

"I'll keep that in mind."

"See that you do." Sierra stared at her for another moment with a piercing look before she spun on a high heel, her sleek ponytail flying in the air, and stalked from the room.

As Sierra's footsteps receded, Julia twisted to face her screen, the confrontation still reverberating in the quiet room. She took a deep breath, trying to steady the unease Sierra had stirred. Her new, ready-made family wasn't something she had fully adjusted to yet.

She glanced over the glamour of the gardens that had served as the backdrop for their wedding photos yesterday. Their future, not just mine, she reminded herself. She would have to be more careful with her actions in the future. Her independence would have to take a back seat for now.

She tried to focus on the blinking cursor staring back at her from the pages, setting her fingers on the keyboard, but her mind drifted back to the conversation with Sierra. She couldn't decide if she admired the young woman for protecting her family or if she was annoyed she was presumptuous enough to assume she was privy to all of Julia's business.

She rolled her eyes as her nostrils flared, with a deep sigh. She stretched her fingers and rolled her shoulders back as she tried to focus on her work. She found herself longing for the simplicity of her old life. It had been that nostalgic pang that sent her scrambling out the door this morning.

Before she could type, a knock sounded at the door.

She expected Sierra had come back to push for more answers about her mysterious phone call that morning. With slumped shoulders, she swiveled, surprised to find Worthington at the door instead.

She stiffened as she offered him a tentative smile. "Worthington, is there something I can help you with?"

"No, it's my job to help you. I came to see if you would like tea, coffee, or anything else before you begin your work."

Julia licked her lips. This, too, was unfamiliar territory. She'd never had someone wait on her before. "Oh, no, thank you."

"Are you certain? Mr. Harrington said you preferred tea, and we have a fully stocked selection."

Julia hesitated, unsure how to respond. She didn't want to be rude, but she felt uncomfortable issuing orders. The man's presence eased her nerves, surprisingly, a stark contrast to the prickling tension that still lingered in the air after the confrontation with Sierra.

"Mrs. Harrington, may I be so bold as to speak frankly with you?"

"Of course," she said, with a shaky breath. Was she about to receive another tongue-lashing, this time from the butler?

He took a few steps closer, his features soft. "This is your household now. You should not feel uncomfortable asking for anything. That includes your breakfast in the morning at whatever time you'd like it."

She pressed her lips together, letting her gaze fall to the

floor. "It seems I caused quite a stir this morning with my disappearing act."

He smiled at her. "Mr. Harrington was very worried."

She nodded. The conversation with Sierra had enlightened her. "I'm sure. I didn't think about how it may look."

Worthington's cryptic smile suggested he disagreed, but he did not press it any further. "Now, about your breakfast…"

"I can–"

"You can, but should you? Unless you hope to take over someone's position on the staff, we would be most grateful to do our work for you."

Heat washed over her. "I'm sorry. I'm not adjusting to this new role very well, am I?"

"On the contrary. I think you have made more of an impact than you know."

Her failings seemed to follow her wherever she went today. "Sadly, the impact seems to leave something to be desired."

"I would argue, while there is much to desire, it's all positive." He smiled at her for a moment before he said, "Tea?"

"Ah, yes, thank you. English breakfast."

"Cream and sugar?" Worthington asked, already making his way to the door.

"Two sugars, no cream, thank you."

"Of course, Mrs. Harrington."

Julia eased back into her chair as he left. That conversation seemed to have gone better than the previous one, though Worthington seemed to give her far more credit than she deserved. The slow chipping away at her independent nature would be a challenge for her over the contract period.

Would she ever become used to this? It was best not to. One year from today, she'd be back in her cramped apartment. She wondered how she'd adjust back to her old life.

With a shake of her head, she dismissed the ruminating. She had enough to focus on other than the loss of grandeur she hadn't yet accepted anyway.

Worthington arrived with a steaming cup of tea. After thanking him, she finally settled in to pen some words. Despite the difficult morning, the words flowed from her once she found her rhythm.

As she typed out the end of her chapter, she sat back with a smile and reached for her cup of tea. She found it empty. It seemed like the perfect time for a break, so she gathered the saucer and cup and headed downstairs to refresh her drink.

"Mrs. Harrington," Worthington said as she descended the stairs, "excellent timing. James has just arrived to take you into town."

She froze for a moment, her mind blank.

"For your lunch with Mr. Harrington."

"Oh, right." Julia cursed herself for forgetting the first engagement with her husband. She was turning into a terrible fake wife. "I just need to grab my purse."

She handed the cup and saucer to the butler as she dashed back up the stairs and flew into her room to grab her purse. A fleeting thought of her solitary lunches at her desk crossed her mind as she glanced longingly at her manuscript.

Those days were gone for the moment, though. She pushed herself to leave the growing comfort of her private suite behind and return to the front door.

James waited outside for her, popping the door open as she stepped into the autumn air. "Mrs. Harrington," he greeted her, with a nod.

"Hi. Sorry to keep you waiting."

"It's not a problem at all." He closed the door behind her before circling around to the driver's door and sliding behind the wheel. "Have you had a productive day?"

"Uh, so far, yes," she said as the car slid down the driveway. "Thank you."

He smiled at her, flicking his gaze to the rearview mirror. "I'm sure Mr. Harrington will be pleased to see you."

The statement stabbed at her gut. She supposed she'd have to get used to this. Everyone else would assume they were truly married. She'd have to field these types of statements over and over. She smiled this one away and replaced it with a question for the driver.

"How long have you worked for Mr. Harrington?"

"Twelve years."

"Wow, that's quite a long time," she answered. Grant Harrington must not be a bad employer. His staff seemed exceptionally loyal to him.

"Mr. Harrington's an excellent employer, and a heck of a guy."

Julia slid her gaze to the buildings that filled in around them as they entered the city. The stark change mirrored the chaos of her life. She drummed her fingers against the door as the tall silver building of Harrington Global came into view.

James eased to a stop at the curb and hurried around to open her door. She stepped out, her neck craning to stare up at the tall building.

"Top floor. Straight back to Evelyn," James whispered to her, with a grin.

"Right," she said, with a nod. "Thanks."

Shoving aside any misgivings, she crossed to the door and tugged it open. A security guard sat at the desk. She approached it, biting her lower lip as she waited for him to pull his eyes from the screen he watched.

"Help you?" he said before he glanced up.

"Uh, yes, I'm here to see Grant Harrington."

"Do you have an appointment?" he asked, blindly reaching for a clipboard as he scanned the list.

"Umm, yes?" she said, with a question in her voice.

"Name?"

"Julia St...." She stopped before she corrected herself. "Julia Harrington."

The man snapped his gaze up, studying her before he set the clipboard aside with a clatter. "Mrs. Harrington, I'm sorry. I didn't see you come in."

He skirted the desk and crossed to the elevator, poking at the button.

"That's okay," she said with a smile as the doors whooshed open.

The guard reached inside after she entered the car and pressed the button on the highest number. "You have a lovely day, now, Mrs. Harrington."

"Thanks, you, too."

As the elevator tugged her up, she reflected on the reaction. Amazing how people treated you so very differently when they thought you were someone. Julia Stanton never would have commanded that much attention.

The doors opened, and the din of a corporate office in full swing pressed in around her. Julia took a few tentative steps in before she spotted a glass office in the back marked with the name "Evelyn Clarke." She headed for it, hovering at the doorway and clearing her throat.

The woman flicked her gaze up over her reading glasses, arching an eyebrow. "Mrs. Harrington, please come in."

Julia stepped forward, her purse strap clutched tightly in one hand as she offered the other to the woman who rose from her seat. "Hi, I'm Julia, nice to meet you."

"Evelyn, but everyone calls me Evie. Give me one second to tell him you're here. He hasn't stopped since he came in this morning."

Julia offered her a polite smile as she snatched up her receiver and pressed it to her ear, tapping a few buttons.

"I'm sorry to interrupt, Mr. Harrington, but you may have another problem to add to your list."

Julia knitted her brows, wondering what other problems he navigated.

"You'll need to come up with a good excuse for why you forgot your wife was coming for lunch." She grinned up at Julia. "Right away, sir."

"You can go on in." She poked her pen toward the closed office door.

Julia smiled at her again before she stepped toward the door. Had he forgotten to tell Evelyn? Maybe he hadn't expected her to come. She twisted the knob and poked her head into the office.

"Hey, Juls, come in," Grant said from behind his desk. Paperwork covered every inch of it.

Her forehead crinkled at the nickname, though she assumed it had been a rehearsed move to make them seem more familiar than they were in front of the secretary.

"Hi," she said as she stepped into the office.

He rose from his seat, offering her an apologetic smile and sigh. "I'm really sorry–"

"It's okay," she said, sticking close to the door.

He studied her for a second too long. "It's not. I asked you to lunch a day after we're married and cancel on you."

She scanned the paperwork on the desk. "It looks like it's for a good reason."

"You're being too kind."

Julia weighed her response. This polite dance seemed silly. "I'm not," she said, with a chuckle. "We didn't get married to have lunch together. You're saving your company. And this is part of that." She waved a hand over the paperwork.

A slight twinge in his expression confused her before he glanced down at the paperwork. "Right."

She stood in awkward silence for another moment before she said, "Well, I'll leave you to it."

She stepped toward the door when Grant stopped her. "Julia, wait."

As she froze, she flicked her gaze back to him.

"Uh, this can wait. I'm not getting anywhere on it anyway. Lunch will be a nice break."

She offered him a tight-lipped smile and nod when the phone rang. Grant rolled his eyes before he grabbed the receiver.

"Yeah?" Grant listened to whomever spoke on the other end. "Well, tell him I'll call him back." He flicked his gaze to her. "I'm having lunch with my wife."

He slammed the receiver down and skirted the desk. "Let's go."

"You can take the call if you need to."

"Careful, Juls, you're going to give me a complex."

She offered him a demure smile. "Sorry."

"I have a very delicate ego, you know?"

She chuckled as they stepped out of the office. "Evie, hold all my calls. I don't want to be disturbed while we're at lunch."

"Of course, sir. Enjoy your lunch, and Julia, lovely meeting you."

Julia passed along her regards before Grant ushered her out of the office and to the waiting car below. Within fifteen minutes, they were seated along the water at the Garden Terrace, with the warm fall sun shining down on them.

After placing their orders, Julia set her gaze over the water, struggling to come up with a topic of conversation. She flicked her gaze back to Grant, clearing her throat as she tried to make their lunch not look awkward to the casual onlooker.

"Sounds like you're swamped at the office."

"Nothing I'm not used to."

She smiled and nodded as she grasped the edge of her chair.

"And how are you settling in? Everything okay at home?"

She lifted her shoulders in a shrug. "Uh, yes. I wrote an entire chapter this morning."

"Oh, great. Sounds like Harrington House agrees with you."

She offered him a tentative smile as the conversation with Sierra flitted across her mind. She thought of bringing it up, but the arrival of their food stopped her. As she pushed around the crisp greens in her salad, though, she felt compelled to bring it up.

"I–"

Her words were cut off when Grant spoke at the same time.

They shared a chuckle. "Oh, sorry, go ahead."

"No, no, please. You were saying?"

She pressed her lips together, suddenly unsure she wanted to say anything. She swallowed hard as she stabbed at a piece of Romaine.

"I called my sister this morning. Sometimes when I'm stuck on a plot point, it helps to talk it out."

"Oh," he said, the corners of his lips tugging up, "oh, that's...she doesn't mind at that hour?"

"She's used to be woken up at all hours of the night," Julia said, with a shrug. With the weight of Grant's gaze on her she added, "I just wanted you to know. Sierra seemed concerned. I wanted you to know it was nothing to worry about."

His smile faded slightly. "Did Sierra say something to you about it this morning?"

"We had a conversation after you left. I didn't tell her what my call was about, but I did feel you had the right to know."

"I'm sorry she did that. Sierra can be...overzealous."

"She had a point. I wasn't thinking about how this would look–"

"Of course not. You can take a walk, Julia. We just...were concerned, that's all. About you...not the image."

She offered him a dubious smile, uncertain how much was being said for the sake of prying eyes and ears, and how much was real.

They made small talk for the remainder of their meal.

As they finished, Julia wished him a successful afternoon. He strode out of the restaurant, planning to walk back to his office as she collected her purse for James to drive her back to the house.

"Excuse me, Mrs. Harrington?" the hostess asked as she approached.

The oddness of answering to her married name sank in as she answered. "Oh, yes?"

"This was just delivered for you." She held an envelope toward her.

"For me? Thank you." Julia took the proffered item and sank into her chair to open it.

She pulled out a folded piece of paper and flicked it open. A typed message met her gaze, the crisp, black letters stark against the white paper.

The truth will come out tomorrow.

Her heart skipped a beat as she scanned the crowd as though she would recognize the culprit. Someone had just threatened her. And she had no idea what to do about it.

CHAPTER 11

GRANT

The barrage of notifications on his phone, relentless even after a brief lunch, sent a sharp pain threading through his temples. His grip on the device tightened reflexively. Today wasn't the best day to be out of the office, but it had been necessary. At least that's what he told himself.

His control of the company weighed heavily on his image. What better image to project than an adoring husband stepping out for lunch with his new wife?

His mind turned to Julia as he scanned a new email. She'd told him about her call this morning. Sierra had spoken with her about it. His jaw tightened as he imagined the confrontation. Sierra, always a whirlwind of sharp words and even sharper actions, could be overwhelming. Brought up with privilege right from the start, boundaries were an issue with her.

He'd need to address Sierra's overstepping with Julia, but that was for later – after clearing more pressing issues from his plate.

He tugged the door open to Harrington Global, the city's cacophony fading into a muted hum as he stepped into the cool, polished lobby. The security guard bounced from behind the desk to press the elevator button for him.

"Lovely woman, your wife, Mr. Harrington," he said, with a grin.

"Thank you, Steve. I think I've outdone myself." With a winning grin, he stepped into the elevator and let the doors slide closed.

A minute later, he strolled past the productive hum of the upper echelons of Harrington Global employees, most of whom were glued to their screens before he strode past Evelyn on his way to his office. "I see the world blew up while I was out with Julia."

She leapt from her seat with a stack of notes and two more folders. "As always, sir. I have several messages for you, along with two new contracts that were just received by messenger. You're not going to like them."

Grant collapsed into his chair, running a hand through his hair. "What now?"

"Both producers have changed the terms again."

He rubbed his thumb and forefinger across his brows. "All right. Let me see them. And which phone calls actually need returning?"

"The ones with the red check should be dealt with first. Did you have a nice lunch at least?"

He smiled as he accepted the stack of papers. "Yes. Very nice, thank you."

"She's a lovely woman. Very…refreshing and genuine."

Grant broadened his smile. He didn't miss the subtle

word choice, suggesting Julia was a significant departure from the previous pattern of spouses. That boded well for the plan, at least.

"Thanks, Evie. I'd like to think so."

"Let me know what you need as you work," she said with a bob of her head as she hurried from the office, pulling the door shut.

Grant focused on the first message, his mind echoing Evelyn's statement. Evie hadn't liked his last wife, though after the fourth Mrs. Harrington dumped a vase of cold water on the woman because she hadn't properly dethorned the roses, the relationship had suffered. He let his forehead fall into his palm as regret for his previous decisions ate at him.

At least his current spouse seemed to be better received. His smile faded. Too bad it wouldn't last. Like all his marriages.

He picked up the phone, buzzing his secretary, then plunged into a whirlwind of negotiations and paperwork, his afternoon distilled into decisive calls and contract reviews.

A knock interrupted him as the lights glowed to life in the city behind him. "Yeah?" he called without looking up from the contract he reviewed.

"I'm just reminding you of the time, sir."

Grant glanced at his watch before shifting his gaze to Evie, who, despite it being past seven, still smiled brightly. "I'm sorry. I'm just finishing up. Why don't you head home for the night, Evie?"

"If you're nearly finished, I'll wait and take care of those files before I leave."

"Really, Evie, that's above and beyond. Go home, kiss your husband, and relax."

Evie clasped her hands in front of her, a key signal that

she had no intention of listening to him. "I ought to say the same to you. You've got a lovely new bride at home, who is probably dining alone."

The fleeting image of Sierra smashing an expensive vase on the marble floor when he bought her the wrong color car for her birthday passed through his mind. "Worse," Grant said with a chuckle, "she's probably got Sierra to keep her company."

Evie giggled at the joke. "Then I'd say you better hurry with that work. This one's worth the effort to hold on to, if I may be so bold."

Grant offered a fleeting smile, realizing that wouldn't be a possibility. "Right. One last change, and then this can be typed up and sent back to them." He scrawled a note about the percentage of profit distributed to Harrington Global before he flicked the folder shut.

"All right, that's enough for one day."

"The problems will still be here tomorrow," Evelyn said as she collected the folders on his desk and pressed them against her chest as she wagged a finger at him. "Make sure you take care of that lovely wife, so she is still here tomorrow, too."

Grant laughed as he tugged on his suit jacket. "I will, Evie."

He tossed a few unfinished files into his briefcase and snapped it shut before he tugged it off the desk. Evie followed him out to her office.

"Don't stay too late, Evie."

"Only a few moments to settle these. My husband cooked dinner, and I am not missing it."

"Enjoy," Grant said with a smile as he left her behind. He took the elevator down to the ground floor, where James waited with the car.

"Another long one, sir?"

"Always anymore." Grant climbed into the car, and James slammed the door behind him."

As he slid behind the wheel, he said, "Hopefully, soon it'll turn around."

"That's the plan. Did Julia get home okay earlier?" Grant narrowed his eyes as his driver kept his eyes glued to the road instead of giving him the usual glance through the mirror with a nod.

"Ah, yes. Took her straight back to Harrington House after your lunch."

"James, did something happen?"

"Might be best to let Mrs. Harrington explain it."

A knot of anxiety tightened in his stomach. Each possibility that flashed through his mind seemed grimmer. "I don't like that answer."

"I know you don't. But it's at her request."

Grant narrowed his eyes as the city's buildings fell away. He drummed his fingers against the door handle as the miles passed. Tension built at his temples again as he vetted ideas.

"Not even a hint?"

"Almost home, sir."

"Just remember who signs your checks, James," he said, a teasing edge to his voice that threatened to betray his underlying concern.

The corners of James's eyes turned up as he grinned. "Yes, I do, sir, but keeping in good with the missus is never a bad thing."

Grant chuckled at the statement, though he felt anything but lighthearted as they swung into the driveway. Lights beamed up at the house, showcasing its size and style, even as darkness fell over it. He wondered what turmoil awaited him inside.

He hoped he didn't find Julia's bags packed or his new

wife tied to a chair by an overzealous Sierra as James pulled his door open.

He stepped into the house, where Worthington met him immediately to take his briefcase.

"Good evening, sir. How was your day?"

"Tell me what's happening with Julia. James said something happened. Where is she? Is she okay?"

"Mrs. Harrington is upstairs in her suite. She is perfectly fine. We had a slight incident, and I imagine she may still be rattled, though she has put on quite a brave face. A visit from you wouldn't be unappreciated, I'm sure."

"'Slight incident?' I don't like the sound of this," Grant said with a shake of his head as he peered up the stairs.

"The security team is already handling it, sir."

Grant snapped his gaze back to his butler, his stomach flip-flopping again. "Security team? Worthington, what the hell happened?"

Worthington motioned for Grant to follow him into his home office, where Max already waited, his phone pressed to his ear. "Right, well, keep digging. They have to have records somewhere. Fine. Keep me informed." He ended the call and nodded to Grant. "Mr. Harrington, we're doing everything we can to track this down."

"Track what down?"

Max's eyes slid to the butler, who calmly skirted them to approach the desk.

Grant pressed his hands to his temples. "Will someone please tell me what is going on?"

"This afternoon, after you left the Terrace, Mrs. Harrington received this note." Worthington thrust forward the envelope.

Grant snatched it from his hands, slid out the paper, and flicked it open to read the message. He knitted his brows at it as he glanced up at the two men awaiting his response.

"The truth will come out tomorrow? What's that supposed to mean?"

"Mrs. Harrington wasn't certain either."

"Why wasn't I informed of this?"

Max shot a sideways glance at Worthington. "I'm going to continue tracking leads on this. I'll keep you informed."

He scurried from the room, leaving Worthington alone with Grant to deal with the remainder of the conversation.

Worthington clasped his hands in front of him. "Mrs. Harrington felt it was best not to disturb you."

Grant's brow furrowed as he tried to make sense of the situation. His previous wives would have demanded immediate action, parading into his office and making it public knowledge. Julia's discretion was a variable new to his calculated world.

"And you listened to her?"

"She is the lady of the house, sir."

"Well, at least she told someone."

"You may wish to credit James with the discovery. He felt she seemed agitated when she emerged from the restaurant. When he asked her about it, she showed him the note. He thought it best to go to Harrington Global, but Mrs. Harrington would hear none of it."

"Do we have any leads?"

"The team has tracked this to the courier company, based on footage shared from the restaurant, and they are working to find the specific courier who delivered it to question."

"So, we have no idea."

"In short, that is correct, sir."

Grant breathed out a sigh, his hands falling to his hips. "Outside of insisting on not contacting me, how is Julia taking it?"

"The newest Mrs. Harrington seems determined to be as unobtrusive as possible. I detect upset, but she isn't very dramatic. She's tucked herself away in her suite." The barely perceptible flick of Worthington's eyebrows betrayed his surprise at her demeanor compared to his previous wives.

Grant heaved a sigh as he considered the information. Julia was an enigma compared to the women he was used to.

"Shall I let the cook know you're ready for dinner?"

Grant rubbed his chin before he snapped his gaze to his butler. "Give me a few minutes."

"I take it you will visit with Mrs. Harrington first?"

"Yes, and then I'll let you know if she's up to dinner or not."

"Very good, sir." Worthington offered him a nod before he skirted him to leave the room.

Grant spent a minute alone collecting himself. With the conundrum of his new wife, he wasn't certain what to expect or how to approach it. More volatile women were his norm. Had he anticipated a glass tumbler being tossed at his head when he entered the room, he would have been more prepared for the encounter than for the barely visible upset Julia displayed.

With tension building across his shoulders, he left his office behind and climbed the stairs to seek his new bride. He peered through the slightly ajar door into her writing office. She clacked away on the keys, a set of yellow-tinted glasses perched on the bridge of her nose and pencil shoved into a messy bun.

He watched her for a few minutes before he rapped his knuckles against the door jamb.

"Oh, just a second," she called, without ever taking her eyes off the screen. Her fingers deftly sent dozens of characters spilling onto the page before she tapped the period and bit her lower lip as she studied the words for a second before she twisted. "Yes? Oh, hi."

"Hi," he said, with a smile. "Sorry to interrupt."

"No, it's fine," she said, waving away the document as though it didn't matter as she slid off her glasses. "Late night, huh? Did you get everything finished that you hoped?"

His forehead pinched for a moment. She hadn't even brought up the note, instead asking about his day first. "Uh, yes, most of them are, unfortunately."

She bobbed her head up and down as though she understood before she sipped from the water glass next to her.

He took a few more steps into her room, his forehead tightening again. "I heard you had a bit of a rough day yourself."

"Oh, Worthington told you about the note?"

Grant nodded as he pulled a chair from the work table closer to her and eased into it. "Yes."

She tugged her lips back into a wince. "I'm sorry, I don't know…" She paused as she stared at the desk for a moment. "I don't know where that came from, or why it happened."

Was she apologizing for something that happened *to* her? "You don't need to apologize. I just want to make sure you're okay."

She glanced at him with an incredulous look on her delicate features. "I'm fine. I just…the hostess gave me the note, that's all. I don't know what it could mean. I just…it gave me a little panic."

"Julia, why didn't you call me?"

There was that blank look again, as though she didn't understand what he was suggesting. "You were busy at work."

"I'm never too busy for you." The truth in his voice surprised even him.

She seemed taken aback by the words, and he rushed to add, "Are you okay now?"

She offered a fleeting smile and nod. "Yes. I hope tomorrow comes and goes and it was all just a false alarm."

He smiled at her. "Right, which very well could happen. This could be a...sick joke on my new wife."

"Right."

They sat in silence for a breath before Grant said, "Well, if you're up for it, we should head down for dinner."

"Oh, sure, let me just make sure this is saved." She spun to the computer and clicked a few keys.

"Definitely don't want to lose all your work from today."

"No," she said with a soft laugh as she turned back to him. "Ready."

Grant rose from his seat and took her hand to lead her to the dining room.

Sierra sat drumming long, manicured nails against the table. "Oh, there you are. I thought I was going to sit here alone."

"I'm sorry, honey," Grant said, with a kiss on the top of her head, "we had a little emergency."

Sierra arched an eyebrow as she whipped the napkin from the table onto her lap, her eyes trained on Julia. "Oh?"

"Yes, Julia got a threatening note earlier today. You wouldn't know anything about that, would you?" While he kept his eyes trained on his daughter, he couldn't help noticing the crinkled brow of his wife at his words.

Sierra scoffed. "Why would I know anything about that? What did it say?"

"You didn't send it?" Grant asked as the staff set down their plates.

Julia remained frozen, not lifting a fork to dig into her meal.

Sierra scowled at him and offered an icy, "No," before she stabbed her steak and sliced through it with a knife. "Why would I send it?"

Grant shrugged as he picked up his fork and skewered a green bean.

Sierra slid her shrewd gaze to Julia. "Did you tell him I did?"

"No!" she exclaimed.

"Don't blame Julia. Someone sent her a threatening note, and I just wanted to be sure it wasn't you."

"Again, why would I send it? This was all my idea."

Silence pervaded the dining space until Sierra clicked her tongue again. "Well, is anyone going to tell me what it said?"

"The truth will come out tomorrow," Julia answered, finally picking up a fork.

"What truth?"

"We don't know," Grant answered, setting his utensils down as he reached for his wine glass. "Security's tracking it."

Sierra settled her gaze on Julia again. "Is there some secret about you we should know?"

"Sierra," Grant growled, the warning in his voice clear.

"Well, Daddy, maybe there is?"

"The only secret I have is the one that involves you," Julia answered. "Beyond that, I have no idea what that note hints at."

"Let's hope nothing," Grant said.

They finished the meal with the pall of the note lingering. Julia excused herself back to her room following the meal, which made Grant somehow more nervous and less nervous at the same time. He plopped into his desk chair shortly afterward, planning to review a few contracts he hadn't gotten to earlier. He snapped open his briefcase, only to find the files missing.

With a curse under his breath, he let his head fall back against the supple leather of the executive chair. He pressed the button on the phone, waiting for James's voice to answer.

"Yes, sir?"

"James, I need to go back to the office."

"I'll bring the car around."

Grant shook his head. At this hour, he'd drive himself. "Bring around the Mercedes. I'll drive myself."

"Are you sure, Mr. Harrington?"

"Absolutely. Enjoy your evening."

"I'll have the car at the front door in five minutes."

Grant leaned back in his chair and rubbed his neck. If he didn't want to get a jump on these files first thing in the morning, he'd have let them go, but he wanted to make a little more progress before calling it a day.

He loosened his tie and tossed it on the desk before he strode toward the foyer.

Julia wandered down the stairs, with an empty water glass in hand. "Back out?"

"I forgot a file at the office."

She offered him a nod as she rounded the railing and continued toward the kitchen. "Be careful. See you in the morning."

He furrowed his brow at the response. "Thanks. See you in the morning."

Grant's trip took a little over an hour. He arrived back home, reviewed his contract, and collapsed into bed.

The alarm screamed through the still-dark sky the next morning. With a groan, Grant rose from his bed to begin his day. He switched on his television as he buttoned his dress shirt, scanning the market news scrolling at the bottom until something else caught his attention.

The blonde newscaster's eyebrows pinched as she broke the serious story. "Police are asking the public for any information on a sixty-two-year-old woman missing and presumed dead after her car was found abandoned last night near Lake Serenity in Greenhaven Park." A picture flashed across the screen, and Grant's heart skipped a beat. "Evelyn

Clarke was reported missing by her husband shortly after nine pm. Police then found her abandoned vehicle with blood stains. Anyone with information is asked to call the information hotline."

Grant sank onto the bed, flicking off the television as he sat in stunned silence. What had happened to Evelyn, and had he played a role in it?

CHAPTER 12

JULIA

The shrill cry of the alarm shattered the morning's peace, jolting Julia from a peaceful slumber. Within seconds of awakening, the reality of life in Harrington House pressed in around her.

A twinge twisted her stomach as she wondered if anything would come of the threatening note she'd received yesterday.

She swung her legs over the bed's edge, her fingers curling into the plush, luxurious sheets – a stark reminder of the opulent yet hollow world she now inhabited. She agonized over whether her feigned happiness at the wedding had fooled anyone. Had someone noticed the subtle hesitations, the fleeting shadows of doubt in her eyes?

Was that the truth that threatened to be revealed?

Had she somehow already let everyone down?

On top of her already swirling thoughts, the gala loomed

on the horizon. Tonight, under the scrutinizing eyes of high society, she and Grant would debut as a couple. One misstep on the daunting stage could have unforeseen consequences. She feared her abilities would fall short. If they hadn't already.

She rose and plodded to the bathroom, darting back when her phone rang with her heart in her throat.

Her sister's name appeared on the screen. She snatched it from the charger and answered, her voice hushed. "Hi, sis."

"Morning, Juju. No early morning dish session today?"

Julia heaved a sigh as she settled on the edge of the bed again. "No, not today."

"Everything going okay, then?"

Julia's heart skipped a beat. The question lingered in her mind, echoing her own fears. How could her sister, thousands of miles away, sense the facade she struggled so hard to maintain?

"Yes," she said, her voice a bit too high as she forced the words out of her tight throat. "I made such great progress yesterday." She hoped her sister didn't pick up on the tremor of uncertainty in her voice.

A pause sounded on the opposite end. "Is everything okay?"

"It's fine. Perfectly fine."

"Are you sure?" Alicia asked. "You sound…weird."

A hurried chuckle escaped Julia, and she tightened her grip on her device. "Weird?"

"Yeah, weird. You're doing the voice. The 'I'm okay but I'm really not' voice. Are you sure this publishing contract is working out?"

"I'm fine. The contract is…fine. I'm just…working through my book and hoping not to hit writer's block, because I'm on track to have my manuscript to them early, which always looks good, right?" Julia held her breath as she awaited her sister's response, thanking her lucky stars she couldn't see her right now, or she'd probably know she was lying. With no intention of admitting her current circumstances, or her marriage, she hoped the conversation would end swiftly.

"All right, well, I hope your progress keeps up. Call me if you get stuck again."

"I will. Take care, sis."

The call disconnected, and Julia blew out a sigh of relief. She sucked in a breath, trying to quiet her nerves. If she struggled this much two days into this venture, she'd never make it through the entire year.

"Maybe lying gets easier," she murmured as she climbed to her feet to ready herself for breakfast, which would now be made by the staff and delivered to the dining room.

Preoccupied with her thoughts, she moved through her morning routine, dressing before she descended the sweeping staircase, her fingers brushing against the cold banister. The mansion, already abuzz with activity, seemed more fraught this morning. She paused at the foot of the stairs, observing the flurry of activity as she sought out Worthington.

The staff rushed around as though there was a crisis. Her heart rose into her throat. A maid raced past with a pot of coffee. Julia lingered on the bottom stair until she spotted Worthington.

"Mr. Worthington, has something happened?"

"Mrs. Harrington," he said, guiding her toward Grant's private office, "I'm glad to see you."

Her palms turned sweaty as he closed the doors behind her. She glanced around the empty room, which seemed cold and austere before she twisted to face the butler.

"We've had a bit of bad news this morning." The down-turn of his lips suggested his tension.

"Oh, no," Julia murmured, assuming this had to do with the warning yesterday. She wondered if perhaps he'd been asked to deliver the news that her services were no longer required.

"It seems Evelyn Clarke, Mr. Harrington's secretary..." He paused, searching her face for a glimmer of recognition.

"Yes, I met her yesterday."

With a fleeting smile, he nodded. "Yes. Well, it seems she has gone missing and is presumed dead."

"Oh, that's terrible." Julia pressed a hand to her chest as she recalled Evelyn's kind smile just the day before. "Do they know what happened?"

"The investigation is still underway. Understandably, Mr. Harrington is taking it quite poorly."

Julia bobbed her head as her eyes fell on the thick area rug. She wondered if the note she'd received had anything to do with this. "Yes, obviously."

"I wondered if...perhaps he would appreciate a visit from you."

Julia snapped her gaze to the man. Did he really think that would do anything? "Oh, I don't want to disturb him."

"Disturbing him may be the best thing for him."

Julia bit her lower lip before she nodded. "All right. I'll head up now."

"Thank you. And if you could get him to consider eating."

Julia cracked a slight smile. "I'll do what I can, but I'm hardly a miracle worker."

Worthington returned her smile. "I disagree."

He pulled the doors open and motioned for her to precede him. With a tentative glance at him, she crossed to the stairs and climbed up, navigating the halls to Grant's suite. His voice floated from within, and she paused before she finally drove herself to knock on the thick wood door.

"Yeah?" his tense voice called from within.

She cracked the door open and poked her head inside. He paced the floor, with his cell phone pressed to his ear. "Well, find something, then. Now!"

With a huff, he jabbed at the phone to end the call before he flicked his gaze to the door. His expression changed from tense to surprised. "Julia?"

"Hi," she said softly. "Worthington told me the news. I'm so sorry."

He let his gaze fall to his now-dead phone. "Thank you. Look, I'm sorry but…"

His unfinished statement hung in the air as a flicker of genuine emotion flashed in his eyes, his usual confidence replaced with a restless energy. She stepped forward, with a shake of her head.

"There's nothing to be sorry for. I just wanted to offer my support."

He studied her for a moment before nodding. "Thank you."

Worthington's words echoed in her mind, and she shrugged. "Maybe you should try some breakfast."

He heaved a sigh, flicking up his eyes with a half-smile. "Did Worthington put you up to this?"

Heat burned across her cheeks as she offered a soft chuckle. "He may have mentioned it. But he is right."

Grant flicked his gaze to his phone again, his fingers tightening around it. "I have no desire to go into the office today."

"Maybe a day off would be best."

He shook his head. "Unfortunately, the blazing fast pace of the corporate world stops for no one. And I should put on a brave face for the company."

She gauged the response as best she could. "Maybe it would be easier with breakfast?" she urged, concern tinting her voice as her empathy kicked in.

A laugh escaped him, crinkling the fine lines around his eyes. "Persistent, aren't you?"

"I promised Worthington I'd do my best."

He grinned at her. "Well, I suppose I shouldn't let you down." He rubbed at his eyebrows as he blew out a long breath. "Oh, we have the gala tonight, too."

"We don't have to go," she offered.

"Again, we–"

"Should," she said, with a nod. "All right, whatever you think is best."

"I may need to meet you there, I'm one hundred percent certain I'll be late tonight. I have no idea how long it'll take for me to finish my work without Evie's help."

The blank expression in his eyes hit her, and she blurted out an offer. "I can go with you. Type or file or whatever you need. I'm certain I won't be as good as Evie, but I'll try."

"Oh, I can't ask you to do that. You have your own work."

"It's okay. I'm ahead on my manuscript. I don't mind."

He studied her, his eyebrows knit. "All right. Uh, if you don't mind, I think I'll take you up on that."

"I don't mind at all. I'm happy to help. I used to help file things for my sister once upon a time. Besides, it will help me from obsessing over tonight's gala."

Grant's mood seemed to lighten just a tad. "Well, I suppose I should get you to breakfast before I press you into service."

She smiled at him as he collected his suit jacket and donned it before they left the room and made their way to the dining room.

Sierra bounced into the room seconds later, a serious

expression on her features. "Please tell me we know something about this?"

"I've got Max searching for information," Grant answered. "We don't know anything yet."

Worthington hurried into the room with Julia's oatmeal, garnished with fresh fruit, and placed it in front of her, whispering, "Miracle worker."

"You'll keep me posted?" Sierra asked as she sipped at the coffee and waved away the offer of food.

"I will. Where are you off to?"

She grabbed an expensive tote and hurried toward the foyer. "Early morning meeting."

"The gala is tonight," he shouted after her.

"I have plans with friends." Her voice echoed through the pillars separating the rooms.

Grant heaved a sigh. "Nothing stops a Harrington."

Julia managed a few more bites before they left the house behind for the office. The upper floors, vibrant and humming with work yesterday, seemed subdued today as the news spread quickly through the staff.

Grant slipped into his office after a few reassuring remarks to other staff members and collapsed into his desk chair. It seemed the burden already threatened to break his steel nerves.

Julia clasped her hands in front of her, trying to break the tension. "Well, put me to work."

Grant bobbed his head. "Uh…"

"Don't be shy. Just tell me what you need."

Grant mulled it for a moment before he launched into a request. "Okay, uh, I need contract files for several different companies." He passed her a list. "They would be in the filing cabinet by the window. Let's start there."

"All right," she said with a nod, taking the paper and heading for the door.

"Julia," Grant called after her.

She hesitated, hovering in the doorway.

"Thanks."

With a smile and nod, she disappeared from his office and headed straight for the filing cabinet. Within twenty minutes, she'd found all the files and delivered them inside.

"Thanks, Juls," he muttered, his preoccupied mind still focused on the paperwork in front of him. He flicked the folder closed and passed it to her. "Can you update these in the electronic files? Oh, you'll need a password. Use mine."

He scrawled his credentials onto a sticky note and passed it to her.

She retreated from his office and tugged back the wheeled chair neatly tucked in at the desk, her hand touching the cardigan still draped over the back. A sweater the woman would never wear again. Her heart broke for the kindly woman who suffered an unknown fate as she slid into her chair and cleared her throat.

She tapped at the mouse, pulling closer to the desk and crossing her ankles. Her shoe caught something underneath. She wheeled back and glanced under the desk. A large bag lay on its side, with a few items spilled out on the floor.

"Oops," she muttered as she reached for it. Her brows knitted before she touched anything. It looked like a purse. Did she normally leave it here at the office?

Perhaps it was just a makeup bag she kept for quick touch-ups. Julia reached for the strap, tugging it closer as a few more items spilled out, including a wallet and cell phone.

Julia's heart skipped a beat at the detail. Why would her purse be here when her car was in Greenhaven Park?

"Hey, Juls," Grant said, poking his head out the door. He studied her face. "Everything okay?"

She shook her head. "No."

"Did the password not work?"

"It's not that," she said, letting go of the strap as she stood, her heart racing as she steeled herself to divulge the information to Grant. "I found this. I think it's Evelyn's purse."

Grant skirted the desk and glanced underneath. "She kept her purse under the desk, but…"

"What's it doing here if she was in Greenhaven Park?"

"Exactly," he answered.

Fifteen minutes later, she stood in Grant's office as police swept Evelyn's workspace for clues of any kind that could hint at her disappearance. She absentmindedly slid the compass pendant back and forth on the chain as she watched their work unfold.

A warm hand squeezed her shoulder. "Why don't you head home? They won't be finished for hours," Grant said, his voice tickling her ear.

She twisted to glance at him, placing her hand on his. "Maybe you should do the same."

"I'm going to stay. I have a few more things to review. But I'll see you at the gala, right?"

"Are you sure?" she asked.

"Yes, I'll be fine. And I'd like to speak with them when they finish."

Julia hesitated, uncertain she should stay but uncomfortable going home to face her own thoughts. "I can stay if you'd prefer."

He offered her an appreciative smile. "As much as I'd love to have you stay, you should get ready for the gala."

She nodded as she gathered her purse. "See you later."

He kissed her cheek as she stepped from his office and skirted around the crime scene team. As the elevator lowered her to the ground floor, she blew out a long breath. The day hadn't been what she'd expected, and there was still one major event to go. She hoped she had the strength to withstand it.

The doors whooshed open, and she stepped out into the chaos of the city that mirrored the thoughts swirling in her mind. James delivered her back to the estate. She'd have a bit of downtime before she needed to shimmy into the formal gown and head to the party.

Any hopes of slipping into a fictional world were dashed as a pert Sierra paraded her way across the marble floor. "I come bearing gifts."

Julia searched her empty hands, wondering what they could be. "Oh?"

Sierra grabbed her hand and tugged her toward the living room. "Ta-da!"

With a wide grin, Sierra waved her hand at the new picture gracing the wall over the living room. Julia slow-blinked as she stared up at the larger-than-life portrait of her staring into Grant's eyes.

"Well, what do you think?" Sierra prodded.

"It's a bit...large, isn't it?"

"A huge testament to your shared commitment. Nothing says 'I love you' like a massive print of the lovebirds."

Julia's eyes lingered on the portrait as she tried to discern truth from fiction.

"Aww, you're speechless. There's more." Sierra tugged her away from the picture.

"Please tell me it's not cardboard cutouts of us."

"Don't be ridiculous, those are so tacky." She pulled her to a box on the table at the back of the foyer. "Here are the framed desk photos. I'm putting one on Daddy's desk at the office and here at home. You should find a spot on your desk for this. Oh, and you may want to update your socials with–"

"No," Julia said, with a shake of her head. "I don't post on social media, so..."

"Whatever, fine. Just make sure this all looks legit." She

rolled her eyes as she grabbed two of the framed pictures. "And for heaven's sake, don't screw up tonight. Okay?"

Julia heaved a sigh, exhausted already. "Right."

"Have fun, StepMommy." Sierra pounded her way toward Grant's office.

Julia slid her eyes closed, collecting herself for a moment before Worthington's voice jolted her back into reality.

"Mrs. Harrington, welcome home. Would you like a cup of tea before you dress for the gala?"

She nodded, appreciating the soothing gesture. "I'll take it in my office."

She climbed the stairs and collapsed into her desk chair before she set the frame next to her monitor, tracing the outline of her jaw as she smiled up at her husband. The moment looked so genuine, even she couldn't tell the difference.

She hoped that remained true for the rest of the evening. The hour slipped by far too quickly, and before she realized it, she stood in the sapphire blue dress, gazing at herself in the mirror. Her life seemed to be passing by before her eyes faster than she could process it.

A knock sounded, and she pulled herself away from her inner turmoil. Her gown swished around her as she crossed to the door and pulled it open to find Worthington.

"Oh, is it time? I just need to put my shoes on."

"Almost. Mr. Harrington asked me to give you this for this evening. He regrets he wasn't here to give it to you himself." He showcased a velvet box before he snapped it open.

Julia's eyes went wide at the diamond-encrusted sapphire pendant. She flicked her gaze up to Worthington before she ran her fingers over the gemstones.

"This is beautiful."

"He hoped you liked it. He asked me to tell you it reminded him of your eyes."

"I don't think they're this dazzling," Julia said as he lifted it from the velvet and handed it to her. She clasped it around her neck before she hurried to slip into her shoes.

Within minutes, she was tucked in the back of the car and sent off to the ball feeling like Cinderella. Her clock, though, would last longer than to just midnight.

Her heart thudded in her chest as James pulled up to the Astoria Regency. James helped her from the car, and she lifted her skirts as she climbed the stairs to the grand ballroom.

Light music tinkled in the background under the din of chatter and laughter from a party already in swing. Julia stood in the doorway as she craned her neck in search of her husband. Blood rushed through her ears, dampening the noise around her. She spotted him speaking with a senator across the room.

Before she could move, he flicked his gaze to the entrance, his speech stopping mid-sentence, and the corners of his lips turning up. He muttered something to his companions before he strode toward her.

The smile on his lips broadened with each step. She closed the gap between them.

"Hi."

"Julia, you look…"

She glanced down, wondering if there was a problem.

"I didn't think you could outdo that wedding dress, but I was wrong."

"Oh, thank you," she said, heat rising in her cheeks.

"Come on, there are a few people I'd like you to meet."

She nodded as she took his arm. "How was the rest of your day? Did the police find anything else?"

"They said–" Grant began when a flurry of activity sounded behind them.

Julia twisted to find several uniformed police officers pushing through the party guests as they stormed toward them.

They pushed their way between them, sending Julia stumbling back a few steps.

"Grant Harrington, you are under arrest for the murder of Evelyn Clarke."

Julia's eyes went wide, and her heart stopped as the officer rambled on with Miranda rights. Her mind reeled.

This can't be happening.

CHAPTER 13

GRANT

The cold shackles closed around his wrists tighter than he would have preferred as the officer read off the charge.

He huffed out a sigh, disgust laced with an undercurrent of disbelief. A murder accusation was absurd. The publicity stunt had been designed to embarrass him. And when he found the person responsible, he'd sue them out of the country.

His heart pounded a bit faster as one of the officers roughly tugged him toward the door. What if they couldn't untangle this mess quickly?

He flicked his gaze to Julia, who stood stunned a few steps away.

"Julia, go straight home," he called as they led him away.

His last vision of her before they dragged him from the room twisted his gut. Her wide eyes and stunned expression cut through him. His mind, already maneuvering to find a solution to this situation, stuck on that image as they shoved him into the back of a waiting squad car.

He may need to do more damage control after this legal fiasco. He was certain Julia hadn't signed that contract with the assumption her new husband would be accused of murder and arrested less than seventy-two hours after their wedding.

The city's lights streaked past the car window, transforming into a blurred neon line as they weaved through the streets toward the station.

"I want my phone call," he demanded as they hauled him from the back of the squad car and led him into the station.

"You'll get it, Harrington. After you're processed."

The handcuffs dug into his wrists, a biting reminder of his current predicament as they ambled through the sterile, buzzing corridors of the police station for a mugshot and fingerprinting. Afterward, they stuck him in a bleak room with one bare bulb casting a harsh light over the stark, barren walls. He drummed his fingers against the metal table, shifting on the uncomfortably hard chair.

The gravity of the situation settled on him like a heavy cloak. He pictured Julia's stunned face again. It pulled him into a well of introspection he typically avoided.

He closed his eyes, pressing his lips together. With any luck, James had her back at the house by now, and the memory of his arrest would fade. The last thing his image needed was a murder charge *and* a divorce.

A gnawing sensation twisted his gut as an unsettling blend of worry and something else he couldn't place bubbled up. It wasn't just his image at stake here. The gravity of the situation and accusation seeped into his thoughts, along with something unwelcome and unbidden. Thankfully, the door burst open before he had to admit any uncomfortable truths to himself.

A detective strode in, a folder clutched in his hand and coffee in the other. He studied the file for a minute, hovering at the door before he flicked his gaze up to Grant.

"Mr. Harrington, looks like you were about to have a lovely evening. Sorry to have ruined that."

"You could always let me go and forget this ridiculous charade. Tell you what, if you do that, I won't even sue this department for all the wrongs you've just committed against me."

The man offered him a tight-lipped, amused smile as he smoothed his cheap tie and sank into the seat across from Grant. "Can I get you a coffee?"

"No, thanks. You can get me my phone call, though."

"Sure. I'll make sure you get that. But I was hoping we could talk first."

Grant clicked his tongue. "Let's cut through the crap here. I don't want to play good cop, bad cop with you guys. Especially for this."

"Maybe you could enlighten me as to what would drive a man of your stature to murder his secretary?" The calm, casual measure to the detective's voice grated on his last nerve.

Grant frowned at the gesture, intended to keep him off balance and make him anxious. It only served to annoy him. "I didn't. And while you sit here and question me over something I didn't do, the real killer is out there, getting away with it."

The man tugged his folder closer and made a note. "It's interesting you said 'the killer.' We have only up until this point said Mrs. Clarke has been presumed dead. Do you know something we don't, Mr. Harrington? Grant? Can I call you Grant?"

"You can call me Mr. Harrington, and you can get me my phone call. I'm not saying a word without my lawyer present." He infused the same commanding presence he used in boardrooms, but there was a hint of tightness in his voice he hoped the detective didn't pick up on.

"Is there some reason you're so interested in lawyering up so quickly?"

Grant clenched his jaw, his silence the only answer to the probing questions.

"Because, see, here's the thing, Grant. Ah, Mr. Harrington, sorry. I can't help you if you aren't honest with me right now."

Grant shook his head at the desperate shakedown attempt. The way things were playing out, he'd be there all night before they let him call anyone, in an attempt to scare him into saying something they could use to pin this on him.

"Let's start with something simple. Where were you last night, between the hours of around nine-thirty and eleven?"

Grant pressed his lips together.

"Nothing to say?"

Grant didn't answer.

"Is that because you weren't home then? Or…maybe you were with your new wife, what's her name? Juliet?"

"Julia," Grant corrected, not certain why the misnomer annoyed him so much.

"That's right, Julia. Maybe you were with Julia. Then we could just ask her and clear this entire matter up." He cocked his head. "No? Is there some important reason you were not home with your new wife last night?"

Grant heaved a sigh as he rolled his eyes. "This isn't going to work. You're not going to get me to say something you can use against me. Just let me have my phone call."

A knock sounded at the door, and another detective poked in his head. "Jim, one second."

Jim flicked his gaze to Grant, sliding the folder onto the table as he smiled. "Excuse me a second."

He rose and crossed to the other man to discuss something in hushed tones. They were likely trying to figure out how to stall enough with his phone call to get him to talk.

Jim nodded his head, murmuring an, "All right," before he strode back to the table and reclaimed his seat. The metal legs screeched across the floor as he pulled it closer to the table.

"Sorry about that. Where were we?"

"You were trying to get me to say something without my lawyer present so you could twist it into making this ridiculous charge stick."

The man gave him an incredulous glance. "That's not what's going on here at all. A woman is missing and may have been killed, and we're trying to get to the bottom of it for her grieving family. And you may hold key pieces of information to help us do that.

"Now, when was the last time you saw Evelyn Clarke?"

The door burst open before Grant could consider that question. "Don't answer that," Mitchell said. "Detective Mulligan, I'd like a moment with my client."

The detective, clearly peeved that legal representation had arrived, frowned at Grant as he snatched the folder off the table. He leaned closer, his face inches from Grant's.

"If you did this, no amount of money is going to get you out of it."

Grant let out a groan as the door clicked closed. "Thank heavens you watch the news, Mitchell."

The man clicked open his well-polished briefcase. "I don't. I was enjoying dinner with a colleague."

Grant's brow furrowed.

"Julia called." He removed a pen and notepad from his briefcase and flopped them onto the metal table.

At the mention of Julia's name, Grant's stomach tightened

into a knot, an unexpected surge of worry washing over him. "Tell me you can get me out of here tonight."

"That depends."

"On?"

Mitchell flicked his gaze sideways to Grant. "The evidence, and anything you'd said so far."

"Nothing," Grant said, with a flick of his hand. "I said nothing."

"Good. All right, let me see what I can find out. But before I do that, I need to know everything." Mitchell twisted to face him, a flat expression on his face.

"There's nothing to know," Grant contended.

Mitchell's eyebrows raised. "Let's cut to the chase. Did you do it?"

"Mitchell, you can't be serious. You can't think I did this."

"Doesn't matter if I did. What matters are the facts. Now, do you have an alibi? Maybe Julia?"

Grant sank his head into his handcuffed hands. "No."

Mitchel arched an eyebrow. "Where were you?"

Grant sucked in a breath. "I went back to the office. Alone."

The attorney jotted a note on the paper. "James can corroborate that?"

"No. I drove myself." Grant didn't miss the deep sigh from his legal counsel.

"Anything amiss when you were at the office?"

"Nothing that I saw."

"When did you last see Evie?"

Grant pulled the memory from his mind. "Just after seven. I worked late, she stayed. I told her to go home. She wouldn't. I left her there filing and went home for dinner." He cursed under his breath. "I should have insisted she leave with me."

"Was she acting odd in any way?"

"No. She seemed fine. She was fine." Grant stared at the bright light reflecting off the metal surface as he searched every piece of his last memories of the woman for information.

"Okay. Let me see what I can find out. We may need to answer a few questions in good faith."

Grant nodded as the lithe man rose from his seat with his notepad in hand and stalked from the room. Left alone, his mind swirled, parsing through interactions with Evie until his mind fixated on another woman: Julia.

She'd had the presence of mind to alert his legal counsel. Perhaps she hadn't been as shocked as she'd seemed. He hoped to find out later, once this mess was cleared up.

The door swung open, and Mitchell wandered back inside. From the expression on his face, Grant took it the news was not good. With a deep sigh, his legal counsel sank into the chair.

"Well?" Grant asked, annoyance edging his voice.

"It's not good."

Grant slid his head forward as he awaited the news.

"They have a text from Evie, telling her husband she was with you and would be home when she finished with the files you had for her."

"What? That's it?"

"That's enough for now," Mitchell said. "In court we can argue this is all circumstantial, but for now they had enough to arrest you."

Grant let his eyes slide closed as his jaw clenched. "How quickly can you get me out on bail?"

"That'll depend on if I can rustle up a judge and convince them Grant Harrington is not a flight risk."

"I didn't do this. You know I love Evie…loved." Grant heaved a sigh as a rare flicker of emotion coursed through him.

"You've got a fleet of private jets and more money than enough. Let's hope we get a friendly judge."

"Look, I'll cooperate with the police. Tell them anything I know; just get me out of here."

"That may help, but I would strongly advise you not to disclose that you were at the office again last night, with no witnesses."

"What do you want me to do, lie?"

"No, just refuse to answer that part. Say nothing. We'll tell them you last saw her shortly after seven, when you left the office. Where did you go when you left?" Mitchell pressed his pen against the pad again.

"Home. I had dinner with Julia and Sierra."

"And then you went back to the office alone. What time?"

"It was around quarter after nine, I think."

Mitchell puckered his lips as he noted it. "What time did you get home?"

"About ten forty-five, give or take."

Grant's jaw tightened. "That means you have no alibi for the suspected time of death, based on when they found her abandoned car."

Mitchell studied his legal pad for a moment before he nodded. "All right. Let's see what we can do."

He stepped to the door and motioned for the detectives to enter. Two men joined them this time, and they all settled around the table.

"Look, gentlemen, my client is willing to cooperate to ensure Mrs. Clarke's alleged killer is brought to justice. He will admit that he last saw her shortly after seven, when he left the office."

"And where were you until eleven?" Jim asked.

"I've advised my client to keep his whereabouts during those hours private at this time."

Jim snorted, his frustration obvious as he closed his

folder and scooped it off the table. "Then we have nothing left to say. Looks like you'll be spending a night with us, Mr. Harrington."

Grant flicked his gaze to Mitchell, who held up a hand to signal him to remain calm. "I'll see what I can do."

Jim hauled Grant to his feet and led him through the clinical halls to a set of holding cells. After locking him inside, he leaned against the bars.

"I told you your money won't get you out of this."

Grant paced the cramped cell, his agitation at an all-time high. While they wasted their time on this ridiculous power play, Evie's real killer went free.

And his company went to ruin. Along with his marriage, most likely.

He sank onto the thin mattress covering the cot as the springs protested his weight. It took everything in him not to leap up and pace the floor again. He felt like a caged lion. His muscles tensed as his aggravation reached a fever pitch. With his hands tied, he could do nothing to fix any of his situations.

He removed his jacket and loosened his tie, trying to relieve some of the pressure.

Hours passed before he spotted a shadow moving toward him. A uniformed officer stopped at his cell.

"Good news for you, Harrington, you made bail."

He grabbed his jacket and strode to the door to follow the officer through the corridors. Mitchell waited near a desk with paperwork ready for him to sign. He scrawled his name in the spaces before they returned his personal items.

He checked his phone. Two in the morning. "Mind if I catch a ride home with you? I don't know if I'll get ahold of James."

"He's here," Mitchell said as he led him through the halls toward a waiting room.

Grant screwed up his face. Why had his driver waited at the police station all night? The question was answered the moment they entered the large room.

Julia, still in her sapphire ball gown, pushed up to sit straighter. She offered him a fleeting but tired smile as she rose.

"What are you doing here? Why aren't you home?" He pulled his jacket from where he'd draped it over his arm and wrapped it around her.

"Thanks," she said, tugging it closer. "It's freezing in here."

"Julia, you should have gone home."

She shrugged. "I didn't want you to have to stay here all night."

He wrapped his arm around her shoulders as he led her toward the exit.

"I'll be at your house first thing tomorrow to talk strategy. Until then, try to get a good night's sleep. You'll need it. This is going to be a PR nightmare," Mitchell said.

"Right. See you then."

"They stepped into the cool night air and found James, parked in the visitor's lot. "You were supposed to take her straight home," Grant scolded gently as they climbed into the car.

"I follow orders, sir," the man said.

He slid into the seat next to his ballgown-clad bride and side-eyed her. She had more concern than the wives who had supposedly married him for love. Maybe that was the key. Maybe she only cared about the money.

They arrived at the house and shuffled into the dark space. Julia shimmied out of his jacket and handed it back with a quiet "thank you" and "goodnight."

"Julia," he found himself calling, his voice more vulnerable than he'd intended. As she paused to look back, he added, "Thanks."

BET ON A BILLIONAIRE

The simple word carried more than gratitude for him, but it was the only phrase he could utter at the moment.

She offered him a fleeting smile as she climbed the stairs, pulling earrings from her ears as she went. He watched her go, his heart more uncertain than it ever had been.

She'd waited at the police station all night, but she seemed so quiet now. Would Julia withstand the coming storm? Her quietness in the car and now hinted at unspoken fears he couldn't help feeling were the tip of the iceberg.

Would she survive this ordeal? It didn't seem like it would be easy. And the fallout could be colossal.

CHAPTER 14

JULIA

*C*ollapsing into the luxury of her bedroom's armchair, Julia couldn't shake off the cold, uncomfortable sterility of the police station's waiting room she'd left just one hour earlier.

Her entire body ached, a physical manifestation of the whirlwind of fear, confusion, and tension that churned within her. Each thought of the current predicament sent fresh waves of cold disbelief through her veins. She wasn't certain she'd have felt any better after the pressures of the gala. She'd dodged one bullet, only to have it replaced by a more lethal one.

She leaned forward to tug her shoes off her swollen feet. The large sapphire necklace still clasped around her neck swung forward, its weight suddenly like a noose around her neck.

She grabbed hold of it before she reached to unclasp it. As

she settled back into the chair, too tired to shimmy out of the dress, she clutched it in her hand, a symbol of her luxurious new life.

Her fingers brushed the brass compass at her neck, a talisman from a simpler time. Days filled with genuine laughter and simple dreams contrasted starkly with her opulent yet hollow world.

Her eyes grew heavy when a soft knock startled her fully awake. "Yes?" she called out softly.

"Mrs. Harrington," Worthington whispered as he stepped inside, "is there anything I can get you?"

She forced a smile onto her lips. "No, thank you, Worthington. I'm just going to change and go to bed."

"Of course." He hesitated, hovering at the door for a moment. "Ah, Mrs. Harrington…"

"Yes?" she asked.

"I would simply like to thank you for what you did tonight for Mr. Harrington."

"Of course." Her voice quavered, a reminder of how foreign the grand world of butlers and staff still was to her.

He returned her expression before he stepped toward the door.

"Oh, Worthington," she said, crossing toward him. "The necklace. Here, I'd like to return it."

He stared down at the blue jewel in her hand as she held it out to him before he shook his head. "There is nothing to return. It's yours. There should be a jewelry box if you'd like to keep it there. If you prefer it in the safe, just let me know, and I will attend to it in the morning."

Julia stood in stunned silence as the butler left her alone. She dangled the necklace from her fingers, the sapphire gleaming under the soft light, a tangible reminder of the life she'd stepped into. It had to cost a small fortune.

Her eyebrows flicked up. When you had unlimited money, she supposed it didn't matter what things cost. She placed it in a drawer of the jewelry armoire against the wall before she changed out of her dress and into her pajamas. The difference in material starkly reminded her of the dual lives she currently led.

In the solitude of her opulent new home, she was merely Julia, but outside these walls, she played the role of Grant's wife–a role becoming more and more difficult to manage. Had that been the only thing that drove her to the police station tonight?

She bit her lower lip, her arms wrapping tightly around a fluffy pillow to anchor her as she floated in a sea of unrest, exhausted, but too riled to sleep. As she lay in the silence of the room, her mind replayed their brief interactions. Was there a darkness beneath his charming exterior?

She couldn't imagine he'd have killed Evie. The woman seemed devoted to him. He had no reason to do it.

Though, she admitted as another hour passed, she didn't know Grant well enough to know his tendencies. But the idea that he'd murdered her just didn't sit right with her.

She hoped she hadn't been fooled by the glitz and glamour of her new life into protecting a killer. The thought echoed in her mind as she finally drifted off to sleep.

She awoke well after her alarm was intended to go off. Bright light already filtered through the curtains. She glanced at the clock, finding it was already after nine. Her heart pounded as she wondered what had happened to her alarm. The house seemed quiet. Perhaps everyone slept in.

With tension at her temples, the events of the previous night lodged themselves in her brain. She hadn't come to any new conclusions overnight.

She planned to stay close to her suite today, certain the house would be in disarray. She headed to the bathroom, catching sight of herself in the mirror and flicking her gaze away quickly as she tried to move on with her day and not delve into introspection.

When she emerged, a knock sounded at her door. Her heart thudded as she wondered what may be awaiting her on the opposite side.

She inched it open, finding Worthington with a tray. "Good morning. I've taken the liberty to bring your breakfast to you."

"Oh, thank you," she said as she stepped back and opened the door further. "I'll stick close to my room today and stay out of the way."

"You are never in the way, Mrs. Harrington." The genuineness in his voice suggested the truth of his statement.

She licked her lips as he set the tray on the bed, wanting to ask about Grant, but unsure. She opted not to ask, thanking him for the delivery again.

"Of course." He nodded as he stepped toward the door.

She closed her eyes, cursing a part of herself as the words slipped from her lips. "How is Grant holding up?"

Worthington spun to face her, his features betraying the joy that she'd asked. "Tired, but moving forward to fight this absurd charge. He has been with Mr. Caldwell since early this morning."

Julia nodded. "Good. Thank you."

Worthington excused himself, leaving her to her own thoughts as she sank onto the bed to dive into her breakfast. She forced down a few bites before she returned to her thoughts.

Worthington seemed to believe in the absurdity of the charges against Grant. Was that merely a loyal employee, or did he know the man under the suit well enough to trust that he couldn't commit this crime?

Her mind stretched, testing theories, weaving and tearing apart scenarios. The more she thought, the less she knew. She shoved the tray away after a few more bites, unable to stomach any more. She reached for her phone, feeling the cold metal in her hand.

She desperately wanted to call her sister and confess every detail. Maybe she could help her through this uncertainty.

Her shoulders slumped, and she let the device fall into the rumpled duvet. Her sister would tell her what an idiot she'd been to marry this man she didn't even know.

And maybe she had been. Her heart ached as she dissected every glance and word she'd shared with Grant. Each memory offered comfort and fed her fears.

Her mind whirled, threatening to engulf her in a sea of doubt, when a sudden knock pulled her back to reality. Her stomach twisted as she eyed the wooden barrier. With a long breath, she hurried to it. It was likely Worthington returning for the tray.

She tugged it open to find Grant on the other side. "Good morning." He offered her a tired smile.

"Hi," she answered, finding herself suddenly uncertain in his presence.

"May I come in?"

She nodded as she stepped back and motioned for him to enter. He stalked inside, eyeing her rumpled bed and the half-eaten breakfast amidst the mess.

"Breakfast not to your liking?"

"I didn't have much of an appetite this morning," she admitted, her eyes flitting around the room.

When she flicked them to Grant, she found him standing

closer to her than before. Her heart beat a little harder as he came even closer.

"Julia," he said, his voice soft, "I think we need to talk."

She nodded, and he led her to the pair of armchairs across the room. She sank onto the edge of one, tension building in her body. In Harrington House, she found she couldn't predict what would come next.

Grant flicked his gaze to the floor as he leaned forward, his elbows on his knees. He raised his eyes to hers, studying them for a moment.

"I...I don't know where to start." His words faltered, a hint of vulnerability flicking across his eyes.

She licked her lips as she tried to search for the right words. "I know this situation isn't easy, but there's nothing you need to explain to me."

"But there is," he said quickly. "Julia, I need you to know I didn't do this."

She studied his features. His unwavering eyes, the small pinch between his eyebrows. Was he this practiced at lying, or was he being truthful?

"I know we don't know each other well, and I can't imagine what you must think of me right now, but I didn't do this. I need you to know that." As he spoke, a rare crack in his usually composed facade appeared. His usually sure eyes flickered with a shadow of uncertainty.

She stared at him for a moment as the gears of her mind ground through their process. She wanted to believe him. And she supposed she had to trust him. If he lied, that was on him.

She raised her gaze to find his pleading eyes still on her. "I believe you."

Did she detect a slight sag of his shoulders as he blew out a sigh of relief? He swallowed hard as he bobbed his head.

"Good. I really appreciate what you did last night. And I hoped all of that went without saying, but I wanted to say it just the same. I wanted you to hear me say it." He hesitated tapping his fingertips together. "Especially considering that I'm about to ask you, yet again, to support me in this in a very public way."

She cocked her head at his words.

"I'm sorry to ask you this. I know when you signed that contract, this is not what you had in mind, but...I need you."

The words struck her. She'd agreed to help him save his company by salvaging his image, though, and she supposed this counted as just that. "Whatever you need."

His chin dipped a little as he offered a nod. "Good. Mitch is recommending a press conference. We want to get out ahead of this and try to swing back some of the control of the narrative. I'd really appreciate it if you'd stand behind me there."

Julia imagined the flash bulbs and scrutiny. One hundred times worse than the wedding, but one thousand times more important to Grant. Her mind raced as she weighed the gravity of the move. It wasn't the simple support of a husband; it was a statement to the world that she believed in his innocence. Did she?

She had to stop second-guessing. She went with her gut.

"Of course."

His shoulders seemed to release some of the tension they'd held earlier as she answered. He shook his head. "I... cannot express how much this means to me. I'm sure this isn't what you envisioned when you agreed to this."

She offered him a slight smile as they both rose. "I'm sure it isn't what you expected either."

"I'm usually much better at anticipating things, but this..."

She allowed him his moment of reflection.

"Anyway, could you come downstairs with me? Mitchell

wants to go over some things before we make a public statement."

She accepted his arm, and he led her to his private office. Mitchell and Sierra awaited them. Sierra's normally overzealous behavior seemed to be at a fever pitch today.

"Well?" she demanded.

"Easy, Sierra," Grant said.

Sierra flicked her gaze to Julia. "You're doing it, right?"

She nodded as Sierra blew out a sigh. "Good. Not that you couldn't do it. You signed a contract."

Grant flicked her a quick glance. "I'm not certain the contract applies to defending a murder charge. But it's a moot point, Julia has agreed to the press conference."

"That's good. We need to do everything we can to present a unified front and bolster your public image. This case will be tried as much in the court of public opinion as it will be in the courtroom." Mitchell bobbed his head at her, a silent thank you for making his job slightly easier.

"I've already had a statement drafted for you to read. We won't take questions. Hopefully, it'll all be over quickly."

"Where?" Sierra asked.

"That's up to you. The press has already gathered outside the gates. It may offer a more intimate and relatable setting than to stage it somewhere else."

"Fine. When?" Grant asked.

"The sooner, the better."

The discussion continued briefly before preparations began for the press conference to be held within the hour. The tension in Grant's shoulders worsened as his gaze hardened with every second that passed.

Fifteen minutes later, they strode down the driveway toward the waiting press. Julia's heart pounded against her ribs with every step. Cameras snapped, each *click* an invasive reminder of the world's prying eyes. The security team worked to back up the members of the press, allowing Grant, Julia, Mitchell, and Sierra to step just beyond the gates.

Mitchell held up a hand as shouts from the crowd demanded answers. Julia swallowed hard as the cacophony threatened to unravel the careful demeanor she'd practiced.

"Mr. Harrington would like to make a statement to the press regarding the incident with Mrs. Clarke and his subsequent arrest. After that, we will not be taking any questions."

Flash bulbs glared as pictures were snapped and silence fell over the group. Microphones shoved closer to Grant. Julia held her breath as she stood at his side, hoping her trembling was not visible to the cameras.

Grant launched into his statement, already memorized. "My family and I were both shocked and saddened to learn about Evelyn Clarke's disappearance and presumed death. Evelyn was a treasured member of the Harrington Global family.

"At this time, it also became news that I have been charged with the murder of Mrs. Clarke. It is unfortunate that this miscarriage of the justice system is overshadowing the story of a beautiful woman removed from this life too soon.

"While I pledge to do my best to help with the investigation in any way I can, I want to be clear that I had no involvement in this at all. I am innocent of these charges, and the investigation will prove that. That's all I have to say."

Reporters pressed forward, pushing against the security team as they shouted questions.

"We have nothing further at this time," Mitchell shouted over the crowd.

The gates behind them opened, and they turned to enter the sanctuary of private property when one of the reporters managed to break free and rushed toward them.

She hurriedly spoke into her microphone. "Mrs. Harrington, can you tell us why you'd stand at the side of a killer?"

The petite brunette shoved her microphone into Julia's face as her stern face awaited an answer. Julia's heart thudded as she stared down at the woman who demanded answers from her. As her words hung heavy in the air, a knot tightened in her stomach. Her own doubts, echoed bluntly by a stranger's accusation, left her momentarily speechless. Was she truly standing beside a killer?

CHAPTER 15

GRANT

Grant finished with his statement and allowed Mitchell to take over, driving the press back as they returned to the privacy of Harrington House.

Before they could step inside the gates, a short brunette slipped under the arm of one of his security guards and raced toward them. He braced himself for the biting questions she would launch at him, but the woman didn't come toward him.

Instead, she targeted Julia. Her hurried voice spoke into her microphone. "Mrs. Harrington, can you tell us why you'd stand at the side of a killer?"

His stomach tightened into a knot and jaw clenched as the question hung in the air between them. Julia seemed speechless. He reached for her, concerned about her sudden thrust into chaos, as he bit back guilt for involving her in this complex world. If it wouldn't have looked suspicious, he would have whisked her away from the hungry press member.

Before he could wave her away, Julia lifted her chin slightly.

"That's simple," she answered. "My husband isn't a killer, and the truth will come out."

Grant's fists unclenched as he stared in admiration at the woman he'd married. He'd been unsure of her earlier, but he was beginning to learn the strength hiding under her quiet demeanor.

"All right, that's it, this press conference is over!" Mitchell bellowed as the security team finally managed to grab the woman and wrangle her away from his new bride.

Julia's eyes met his as she turned. She offered him a fleeting, barely-there smile before he ushered her ahead of him down the driveway.

They stalked back toward the house as the gates closed behind them. Cameras continued to snap. How would the public perceive their pairing? Would Julia be painted as another of his victims, or would they give her a more sinister appearance?

His arm slid around Julia's shoulders, hoping to offer her some support after the taxing moment. He was surprised to feel her arm slip around his waist for a few steps before they parted, their hands coming together as they finished the walk.

They stepped into the quiet coolness of Harrington House. Worthington awaited them. "I hope it went well, sir. Can I get you anything?"

"As well as it could," Grant answered.

"Extremely well," Mitchell agreed. "Julia, you could not have done better with that question. That is going to go a long, long way."

Julia offered his legal counsel a demure smile.

149

"Yes," Grant agreed, placing a steadying hand against her back, "you did wonderfully. Thank you."

"Grant, we should discuss a few further things, if you have a minute," Mitchell said.

"Sure. I'll be in in a minute." Grant bobbed his head at the man before he returned his attention to Julia. He searched her face for any signs of regret on her part. "You okay?"

She nodded at him.

"We'll talk later?"

"Of course. Take your time. I'll be upstairs."

"Ah, actually, I had something I wanted to discuss with you, if you have a minute," Sierra said.

"Sierra, now may not be the best time–" Grant began.

"It's fine," Julia said with a pat on his arm before she crossed toward his daughter.

Grant watched Sierra loop her arm through Julia's and drag her away. This may be worse than the press conference for his poor wife. He sincerely hoped Sierra did not drive her away, especially as he found himself needing her more and more.

With a sigh, he retreated to his study with Worthington, the familiar scent of aged leather and mahogany enveloping him. Normally, the framed accolades on the walls would give him comfort, but today they did not.

He poured himself a bourbon. "Tell me you have a way to get me out of this now that we've gotten all the public relations nonsense out of the way."

"It wasn't nonsense," Mitchell told him. "That's almost as big a part of your defense as the legal maneuvering. And you should double the amount you're paying Julia after the last twenty-four hours. She's gone above and beyond for your personal image. Her lack of hesitation and short but clear statement shut that woman down."

Grant stared down at the reflective surface of his liquor,

studying the distorted image of his face. Was she that good at playing a role?

"She has been fantastic."

"She certainly has been. Now, in terms of your defense, I'm meeting with the district attorney in one hour. I'll see how far they're planning to go with these charges. It could be a scare tactic. It could be more."

"These charges are ridiculous. I want them dropped immediately," Grant answered as he sank into his seat.

"I'll do my best to argue that. They don't even have a body, so a murder charge is a stretch." Mitchell grabbed his briefcase and stepped toward the door. "I'll see what I can do."

"I'm counting on you, Mitchell. You've gotten me through some rough waters before."

Mitchell nodded. "You know I'll do everything I can, Grant. We've weathered storms before. We always hit shore."

"Thanks, Mitchell," Grant called as he disappeared from the room. They'd always made it through before, but what would be the cost this time?

He sighed and settled back, the supple leather of his chair creaking under him. These baseless and absurd charges threatened his freedom and the empire he'd built. The thought of it all crumbling due to a fabricated accusation made his stomach churn.

"What a mess this is."

"Is there anything I can get for you, Mr. Harrington?" Worthington asked.

"No. I'm going to try to get some work done."

Grant flicked his gaze over his front lawn. The snarl of reporters still waited at his gates. Grant felt a mix of indignation and vulnerability. Public scrutiny was a familiar game, but the rules had suddenly changed, and now the stakes were both his legacy and life.

His mind reverted back to the moment Julia had answered the reporter. It brought him a slim measure of comfort to have her in his corner.

"Of course, sir. If you need anything, please call."

Grant nodded at him as he spun to face his computer monitor. He tapped the mouse before he waved a hand at Worthington.

"Actually, Worthington, there is something."

The man spun from the door, clasping his hands in front of him as he awaited the order.

"Check on Julia." He tugged a corner of his lips back. "She's with Sierra. Make sure she's still alive and sane, please?"

Worthington offered him a grin. "I will check on her and report back, sir."

"Thank you."

Grant focused his attention on the screen, clicking through his emails without really seeing them. Tension built at his temples. Evelyn usually screened these for him.

He sucked in a deep breath as her loss hit him again. The moment was short-lived as the doors burst open. He hoped to see Worthington with a report on Julia, but instead Sierra paraded into the room, smiling at her phone as she walked.

"Ohhhh, Daddy, my plan is working wonderfully." She squealed with excitement before she spun to face him, her ponytail flying.

"What plan?"

Sierra's shoulders slumped as did her features, her annoyance plain. "With Julia, duh."

She flipped her phone around to show him the screen.

"She's flipped the script. You've gone from..." Sierra swiped at her phone to bring up his mugshot on an early morning news report, "Grim Grant, Billionaire behind Bars, to..."

He rolled his eyes at the headline as she flicked at the screen again. Grant stared at a close-up image of their clasped hands through the gate.

"United Front, From Grim to Grateful, Billionaire Bride Sparks New Narrative."

Sierra turned the phone around to stare at it, her grin broadening. "It's on *all* the networks."

She shifted her screen and swiped through several reports. Pictures of Julia's arm around him, their clasped hands, her head tilted slightly toward him with his arm around her flitted by on the screen.

"Harrington harmony, public opinion shifted as billionaire's wife speaks out. Billionaire bride backs him up. This is perfect."

Grant let eyes fall from the screen to the polished mahogany below his fingertips.

"Why aren't you smiling?"

"I'll smile when Mitchell gets these charges dropped."

"I know this is hard, but look on the bright side. Until the charges are dismissed, at least your image isn't taking a hard hit."

Grant tugged a pen from the cup and turned it over in his hands. "Thanks to Julia."

"Right?" Sierra said, her eyes going wide as though she was stunned. "Who knew? I mean, who could have predicted she'd be *this* good? It's almost like she's a real wife. Actually, no, your previous wives would have headed for the hills by now. Including Mom."

Grant heaved a sigh, groaning as he leaned forward. "You don't have to remind me."

His mind wandered to his string of past, failed marriages, a series of arrangements he'd come to understand lacked any of the depth he'd already found unsettlingly present with his current spouse. He couldn't help comparing the superficial bonds of his past to the complex connection that seemed to grow steadily now.

He recalled when even a whiff of insider trading charges was whispered during his second marriage. His wife hadn't stood by him; she'd sued him to try to nullify the prenuptial agreement and cash in on him before any assets were touched.

"I guess it pays to pay someone to stand by you, huh?"

Her words, her usual blend of sarcasm and nonchalance, reminded him of the heated argument they'd had last summer over her reckless spending. But this time, her words echoed his exact next thought. Her support, the deciding factor in his public image at the moment, was nothing more than an act on her part. It was all a facade, hidden under a contract. She said she believed him, but did she?

His phone rang, jarring him back to reality. He snapped up the receiver, hoping it was good news. "Grant Harrington...no comment." He slammed the phone down onto its base. "Vultures."

"Take it off the hook, Daddy. There's no reason to deal with that now."

"I need to be available for business calls, Sierra. Harrington Global doesn't stop moving because I am in crisis."

Sierra grasped the corners of the desk. "You are Harrington Global, so it should."

"Not for long if we don't get this mess sorted out."

"You'll figure it out, Daddy. I believe in you." Her phone chimed, and she straightened as she glanced down at it. "Gotta run. Bye, Daddy."

"Sierra, where are you–" Grant began as she flitted out the door, the red bottoms of her designer shoes visible as she hurried. "Going."

He pressed his lips together as the question went unanswered. He tugged over a few folders and flicked them open, though he found himself unable to concentrate. The emotional strain of the past few days settled around him, tightening his shoulders.

With a huff at himself, he closed it and shoved it across the desk. He couldn't concentrate. He rose from his chair and stalked to the drink cart, tugging one of the crystal decanters from the mix and pouring himself a drink.

He took a sip, finding little comfort in the hints of vanilla that tickled his tongue. With a glance at his watch, he wondered when he'd hear from Mitchell. Maybe it would all be over.

With another sip, he discarded the tumbler on the desk. It brought him no comfort this time. Instead, his mind focused on one thing, and one thing only he yearned for: Julia.

He weighed it in his mind. Should he seek her out? Would she find him an annoyance? Perhaps he'd taken enough from her already today.

He hadn't heard from Worthington yet, though. He should check on her. He left his drink behind and emerged from his office, his eyes floating up the grand staircase.

Would he find her upstairs in her room? He'd try there first. He climbed the stairs and navigated the halls to her suite.

He spotted her through the open door to her writing office. She bent over a notebook, scribbling madly into it.

He swallowed hard, his resolve suddenly fading. With a step backward, he toyed with the idea of retreating to his office. Instead, he reversed course and rapped against her door.

She twisted to face him, seeming surprised. "Grant. Come in."

He strode toward her, pulling a chair closer as she slid her work away from him. "Making good progress with the novel?"

She glanced at the papers before she returned her gaze to him. "Something like that."

He narrowed his eyes at her. Something about what she said and the flicker in her eyes made him think she was dodging the question. What was she keeping from him?

"Have you heard anything from Mitchell?"

"No," he said, glancing at the neatly laid hardwood beneath their feet. "I'm sorry, I'm disturbing your work."

"No, it's fine. You're not interrupting anything."

He heaved a sigh as he nodded at her. "Julia...I...I can't thank you enough for what you did today and last night. To be honest, you've been...exceptional since the news broke. I just wanted to thank you."

Her features softened as she reached for his hand. Before they could connect, his phone rang, interrupting whatever moment bloomed between them.

"Sorry," he said, pulling it from his pocket. "It's Mitchell."

She sucked in a breath as he hit the answer button and toggled on his speakerphone. "Tell me something good."

"Afraid I can't do that, Grant. The DA isn't backing down. This is going to get worse before it gets better."

Grant's stomach tightened into a knot at the words. His bright future teetered on the edge of a precipice.

Julia's hand finally reached his, giving it a squeeze. It marked the one bright light in the sea of darkness that threatened to drown him. He glanced up at her, certain he wasn't masking the genuine fear in his eyes. How much would he lose?

CHAPTER 16

❧

JULIA

Julia bit into her lower lip as Grant strode toward her, tugging a chair with him before sinking into it.

"Making good progress with the novel?"

She glanced at her notes, her pulse quickening. Her hurried scrawl was far from the novel she was supposed to be working on, but she couldn't explain it to Grant. Her eyes flicked up to meet his, a mix of apprehension and secrecy in them.

"Something like that."

He narrowed his eyes at her, assessing her again. Was she that transparent?

"Have you heard from Mitchell?" she asked, trying to put an end to his questions before she fibbed anymore.

"No." He let his eyes sink to the floor. "I'm sorry, I'm interrupting your work."

She sensed the tension building again in his shoulders, noticed his clenched jaw.

"It's fine. You're not interrupting anything."

He sighed, his head bobbing as his eyes flickered with a vulnerability she hadn't seen before. He seemed to be searching for words. "Julia...I...I can't thank you enough for what you did today and last night. To be honest, you've been...exceptional since the news broke. I just wanted to thank you."

The flicker of genuine gratitude seemed to pass through his eyes. She reached for his hand, trying to offer him some comfort and reassurance when his phone rang.

He apologized, digging it from his pocket. "It's Mitchell."

A knot tightened in her stomach, a tumultuous mix of hope and dread. She wanted the news to be good, not just for the sake of their contract, but because she found herself genuinely concerned for Grant's plight.

"Tell me something good," Grant answered.

"Afraid I can't do that, Grant. The DA isn't backing down. This is going to get worse before it gets better."

A cold sensation washed over Julia, her chest tightening as if an invisible weight pressed down on her. They'd married to improve his image. It had only gotten worse since she'd been around him. Instinctively, she reached for him, squeezing his hand.

When he glanced up at her, she spotted raw emotion, maybe even fear in his eyes.

"I'm heading out to the house. We'll talk strategy this afternoon," Mitchell said.

"See you when you get here." Grant ended the call, his hand still gripping hers as he stared down at the darkened device. After a second, he spoke. "Well...seems like..."

"Grant," she began.

"Julia," he interrupted, "I–"

"Don't panic," she said. "Maybe it's not as bad as it seems."

Grant's face contorted briefly, a glimpse of turmoil flashing in his eyes before he mastered his expression. "Right. Well, I should leave you to it." His voice betrayed a hint of disappointment, or perhaps relief; Julia couldn't discern which.

"I'm happy to wait with you until Mitchell gets here."

He rose from his seat and pushed away the chair. "No, it's okay. You're working."

Julia knitted her brow at the sudden about-face. He seemed to be reeling. Whatever she'd said to him hadn't helped. Maybe she should just stay out of it.

"Good luck with Mitchell."

"Thanks," he murmured, his voice trailing off as he lingered for a moment, his eyes noticeably not on her. Abruptly, he turned and left the room, leaving her alone.

Her shoulders slumped as she studied his retreating form. She tugged a corner of her lips back as she swiveled back and forth in her chair. She supposed he hadn't asked her to offer her support emotionally. He'd hired her to play a role only. Maybe she should stick to it.

Her mind wandered back to her earlier conversation with Sierra. The woman had dragged her away after the press conference to the living room.

Julia stood under the massive picture of their wedding day as Sierra tapped on her phone for a second before she flicked her a narrow-eyed gaze.

"Just making sure we're all on the same page here."

Julia knitted her brows. "What page is that?"

"My Daddy needs support. Things could get bad. *Very* bad." Sierra's voice carried a thinly veiled warning. "I need to know you're going to do what we're paying you to do."

"I'll do whatever is needed," Julia said, her voice steadier than she felt. Sierra's pointed words struck a nerve, reminding her of her transactional nature.

Sierra studied her again. "Good. You've been doing a good job so far. Keep up the good work." Her phone chimed again, and she checked it before firing off a text. "Gotta run, Stepmommy."

Julia heaved a sigh as the conversation replayed in her mind. Maybe Sierra had seen the subtle hints of genuine concern in her eyes. Had she meant to put Julia in her place? To remind her she wasn't part of this world?

Julia pressed her lips together. The interaction with Grant moments ago had certainly cemented that in her mind.

She wasn't a part of this family. She was part of the staff, hired for a role. She'd try to remember that in the future.

With a hard swallow, she pulled the notes she'd been working on closer. She clicked her pen when a knock at the door drew her attention.

She twisted to find Worthington. "Mrs. Harrington, may I bring you some tea?"

"That would be very nice, thank you."

"I'll retrieve it right away." Worthington paused, turning back to her. "I couldn't help noticing Mr. Harrington visited. He was quite concerned about you."

Julia paused, a flicker of surprise twisting her features. Was Grant's concern genuine, or just another part of the facade?

"Yes, he stopped by."

Worthington's expression clouded for a brief moment before it returned to his pleasant demeanor. "I'll be right back with your tea."

Julia sat for a moment, staring at her blank computer screen as she processed the statements. Her mind swam, her thoughts threatening to drown her. From Sierra's insistence about reminding her she was the hired help to Worthington's insinuation that she was more, she couldn't keep track of what was happening.

Her life had been simple once upon a time. It felt like forever before it would be simple again. Less than one week into their contract, she struggled with everything, including her own emotions.

With a sigh, she returned to her notes. She'd lose herself in the logic, hoping it helped steady her nerves.

Julia's fingers hovered over her notes, her mind a battle-ground of duty and emerging personal concern. She was meant to provide a shield, but she found herself entangled in a web of genuine worry and unexpected empathy.

She stared down at the paper, reviewing what she'd already noted.

Timeline? Missing car, no body. Blood–how much? Purse still at office.

Something wasn't adding up to her. Not only had Grant's insistence on his innocence swayed her, so did the facts.

A steaming cup of tea slid onto her desk. She thanked Worthington before he disappeared and grabbed the cup. After a sip of the sweet, hot liquid, she tapped her pen against the page.

Who would have motive?

She couldn't answer that question. She didn't know enough about this world even to begin to answer it. She'd have to work this at another angle. She jotted one single word on the page.

Why?

Why would someone murder Grant's secretary?

She drummed her fingers against her thigh as she chewed her lower lip. This was nothing like a book plot. As a mystery writer, she'd created hundreds of scenarios for murder from personal to professional. Any of them could apply here.

She sucked in a breath. She wasn't making any progress. She'd been in this position a few times before on her own plots, and she'd always reached out to Alicia. She couldn't do that now...or could she?

The corner of her lips turned up as she reached for her phone. She'd wrap the story in the trappings of her latest mystery novel plot and see what Alicia had to say. A former FBI agent's perspective could give her what she needed to piece together more details.

She pressed the call button next to her sister's name and waited while the phone rang on the other end. Her pulse thrummed at a fast pace with each ring as she considered lying to her sister.

"Hey, Juju," Alicia's voice answered.

The sound of ringing phones in the background told her Alicia was at the Harbor Cove Police Department. "Hey, sis. Are you busy?"

"Swamped juggling Harbor Cove's usual crimes–Mrs. Kline's missing cat and Ellie's too-tall gnome. What's up?"

Alicia chuckled, and Julia forced out a laugh to match, her mind comparing her former life with her current one. As Alicia tracked down wayward cats and settled neighborly disputes, Julia worried about her husband being convicted of murder.

"Are you okay?" Alicia asked.

Julia pulled herself from her reflection. "Yeah, umm, I had some plot questions. I can call back."

"No, no, it's fine. I'm going to take my lunch break. I'll leave all the hard stuff to Ethan."

Julia pictured her brother-in-law, now the chief of police in their small seaside town. "How is he?"

"Good. Giving me the evil eye from across the office

because I'm not handling the gnome dispute again. Give me two seconds."

The sound of phones ringing amplified, and Julia pictured her sister moving through the small office to the break room. The noise died down as a door thudded closed.

"Okay, I'm all yours. What do you have? Trouble with a witness? That finicky one we just talked about. What was his name?"

"Uh, no, I'm moving right along with that book, but I had another idea, and I'm trying to flesh it out."

"Oh, wow, your creative juices are flowing, aren't they?" A wrapper crinkled.

"Are you eating a candy bar for lunch?"

"No," her sister murmured as she chewed. "I'm eating a cookie, *then* a candy bar."

Julia traced the question mark on her page, a pang of longing for her old life shooting through her.

"So shoot, whatcha got, little sis?"

"Ummm, right. I have a weird situation, and I wanted a fresh perspective. Picture this: Blake, a public figure, wrongly accused of murdering his secretary. No body, just an abandoned car and some blood. What's your take?"

"Sounds far-fetched without a body. How much blood are we talking about here?"

"How much would it take to be certain she's dead?"

"Massive amounts. Like, tons of blood. The bloodiest crime scene you've ever seen in order for death to be assumed. You remember that crime scene from Riverfield?"

"Yeah?"

"Way more than that."

Julia jotted down the note. "Okay, umm, okay I'm not certain how much blood yet."

Alicia cackled in her ear. "Well, it's your story. You withholding information from yourself?"

"I haven't vetted through all of this, Alicia. I'm just trying to see if this story can even get off the ground."

"Okay, sorry. Keep going. Mr. Blake is accused of murdering his secretary. He has an alibi?"

"No, he was alone at the time of the supposed murder."

"Motive?"

"None. They had a good relationship. What I'm trying to work out is, if he is accused of murder, how would he figure out what happened? Oh, the other clue I have so far is, her purse was found at the office. She'd stayed late with Blake, and he'd left her there filing papers. She texted her husband and said she'd be home as soon as she finished up with him. They found her car abandoned later, the unknown amount of blood, and charged Grant."

"Who's Grant?"

Julia's heart leapt into her throat and she swallowed hard as heat washed over her. "What?"

"You said they charged Grant. Who is Grant?"

"Oh," Julia said, expelling a breath and chuckling more than she should have, "Blake. Sorry...still picking character names. They charged Blake."

The chair creaked on Alicia's end. "I'm still not liking this. The charge feels bogus and overblown. All the evidence is circumstantial, there's no body. This feels clichéd."

Julia scribbled down the notes. "Okay, here's a bit of backstory. Blake's company, which is big, has been in some turmoil. He's been fighting to keep his position as CEO from a hostile board."

Alicia clicked her tongue. "Okay, I see where you're going with this."

"Where?" Julia asked. "With that information, what does your cop mind say?"

"Says someone is out to get Blake and this is a set-up. Likely a crooked cop and a DA in someone's pocket. That's the only way these charges hold up. Otherwise, you'd never get that to stick."

Julia wrote the word "setup" on her sheet and underlined it three times. "Okay, so the plot makes sense if this is some sort of setup."

"Right. Ruin his image, oust him from his position. Ohhh, here's a twist for you...the secretary is behind it."

Julia tried to picture the kindly woman she'd met being the culprit behind Grant's troubles at the company. She shook her head, silently disagreeing.

"So, don't make it her, fine, it's your story." Her sister recognized her hesitance as disagreement.

"Right. Okay, I think...I think that's it for now." Julia scanned her notes. "No wait. How do you prove any of this? How can Grant...Blake get out of this?"

"Look for connections between his board and the cops or DA, find inconsistencies in their story, and follow up on them. If this is a setup, there's proof. Look at the crime scene. Figure out why they staged it the way they did. If this is all fake, there's proof somewhere."

Julia wrote the last two words on her paper. *Proof somewhere.*

Her mind whirled as it stretched to consider how she could track information. She wrote mystery novels, she didn't solve crimes herself. Her characters did, but they often found themselves in hair-raising predicaments tracking evidence.

She bit her lower lip, considering for half a second confessing to her sister. She shook the idea from her head quickly. She didn't want to hear the lecture on a decision she still wasn't certain about herself.

"Go work on your plot, kid," her sister said. "I can practically hear your gears turning from here."

Julia's lips curled at the statement. "Okay. I'll call you if I need more help. Thanks, sis."

"You're welcome. Love you, Juju."

"I love you, too. And give Ethan a hug for me."

"Will do. Take care." The line clicked as her sister ended the call.

Julia stared down at her notes, her eyebrows knitting. Was someone setting Grant up for murder?

CHAPTER 17

GRANT

"*T*ell me you've got this figured out," Grant said as he stormed into his office and went straight to the sleek, chrome drink cart in the corner to pour himself a whiskey.

Mitchell rose from his seat as Grant passed him and shook his head. "We've got some options, but it's going to be tricky going forward right now."

Grant scoffed before he sipped the liquor. "Not what I want to hear."

"I know it's not, Grant, but we're just going to have to sit tight and try to work whatever angles we can."

Grant whipped around to face him, his jaw clenched. "So, they're not dropping the charges?"

"Not even close. In fact, they're thinking of upping them." Mitchell set his expression. "First-degree murder."

"You're joking."

Mitchell shook his head. "I'm not. They're going for premeditated here."

The word "premeditated" echoed in Grant's mind, along with flashes of his future crumbling–the boardroom battles, the public's scorn, Julia's disappointed gaze.

"Based on what? We've had no issues in the past. No public arguments. Nothing."

Mitchell sank into the chair, tossing a folder onto Grant's desk. "Evidence seems flimsy, but they're going for the angle that you've been under extreme pressure."

"And I snapped. Second degree, I can see. It's a stretch, but less of one than premeditated." Grant collapsed into his chair as his temples twisted a notch tighter.

"They claim, based on their investigation, you've made several threats to her. She's feared for her life."

The tumbler rattled against the desk as it slipped from Grant's hands. The clink of the glass against the mahogany echoed his unspoken fears of prison bars and orange jumpsuits.

"Oh, come on. That's ridiculous."

"Still. Grant, have there been incidents where you've lost your temper with her, particularly in the presence of other employees who could testify to this."

Grant sank his head into his hand as the other one flung into the air. "I don't know, maybe. I'm...passionate sometimes."

"That passion may be construed as volatility." Mitchell's voice took on a rehearsed tone as he recited back his conversation with the DA. "They claim they have evidence of increasingly erratic behavior. That it's been documented at board meetings. Even if it's circumstantial, they're spinning a narrative that you've been a powder keg waiting to explode."

Grant settled back in his chair, with a sigh of disgust. "What about the angle that there's no body?"

"DA maintains that it's just a matter of time before it's found. They're dredging the lake and searching the woods."

Grant bit into his lower lip as his eyes slid closed and a curse escaped him. "Mitchell, you've got to do something about this. I can't have this hanging over me going into this battle with the board."

"I know that," Mitchell said, rising and crossing to pour himself a brandy. "Right now, we need to focus our energy on these charges. Bogus or not, they're pushing this through. The DA is up for re-election and looking to make a name for himself."

"Can we use the re-election angle? Does he need a contribution?"

Mitchell took a sip of his drink as he shook his head. "No. And he wouldn't take it anyway. He's running on being a law-and-order candidate. You know, he prosecutes the poor and rich just the same." Mitchell paused, eyeing Grant. "Even Grant Harrington isn't above the law."

Grant scoffed. "Since when has justice been blind?"

Mitchell cocked his head.

"Great," Grant growled, clasping a fist in his opposite hand. "So, we've got a DA looking to use me as a poster boy for his campaign. That's just perfect."

"We'll try to fight fire with fire. They'll have an uphill battle without the body, but the other evidence can make this…difficult."

Grant let his eyes slide shut, frustration building as the fear of going to prison for a crime he didn't commit rose. "Tell me we'll win this."

Mitchell tugged his head to the side, with a half-shrug. "I'd love to. But you know I can't do that. We'll go at it with everything we have." He settled into his seat with another sip of his drink. "We're going to need character witnesses. If they're going for an attack on your persona, we'll need people to refute that image."

Grant rubbed his lips. "Worthington, Sierra."

"We can use them, though Worthington's on your payroll."

"So are the people they're using against me. Though not for long, if I can help it."

Mitchell flicked up his gaze and shook his head. "Do not make any personnel changes during this. After you're cleared, fine. Heads can roll. Before then? It'll only make things worse. As could Sierra. She's a wild card, and she doesn't have the best track record."

Grant rubbed his face as he recalled a speeding ticket Sierra had pleaded with the traffic court judge over, stamping her feet and shouting that she *had* to exceed the speed limit because she'd wanted to get to a new leather handbag at the Gucci store before a friend.

His heart sank as his chances at beating this charge slipped through his fingers.

"What about Julia?" Mitchell asked, his pen pressed to his legal pad.

The sound of her name snapped his attention to the man. "What about her?"

"We can use her as the lead on character witnesses. She's not on your payroll, she's willingly chosen to spend her life with you–"

"That's not entirely true," Grant said with a sigh as he slouched further down in his chair.

"Tell that to the reporter she neatly backed down. She's been the only thing to change the narrative of this story so far. We'd be stupid not to use her."

Grant shook his head as he imagined her on the stand. This had not been at all what he'd envisioned when he'd first laid eyes on her delicate features in the nightclub last week.

"I really have no idea. I didn't choose him. He paid me to pretend to love him."

"Look, Grant, to anyone out there looking in, she chose to marry you. She picked you to spend the rest of her life with. She has an inside track on what makes you tick, on how the stress has been affecting you, on whether you've been volatile, or she's seen signs of you cracking."

"But she doesn't know any of that," Grant argued, heat entering his voice.

"We will coach her," Mitchell said, his voice taking a measured tone.

"And what about the money issue?"

"No one knows after your divorce, she will be paid."

"No, not that. The argument can be made that she married me for money, not love."

Mitchell settled back into his chair, kicking his ankle onto his thigh. "I'm sure the DA will make that argument, yes. We'll coach her. Grant, she comes across as one of the most genuine people I've ever met. She's poised, she's quiet, she's intelligent. This isn't one of your former wives getting on the stand; this is Julia."

He rubbed his temple with his finger. "I'll think about it."

"You'd better think fast. They want a preliminary hearing in the next day or so, pending where they are with their investigation. And if we're using her as a character witness, we want to get her prepped and ready."

He stared at the empty chair next to Mitchell, imagining Julia there as Mitchell put her through the grueling process of preparing to twist the truth on the stand. A twinge of guilt knotted his stomach. His choices had unfairly dragged her into a nightmare.

He leapt from his seat, pacing the floor in front of the large window. "And you think parading Julia into court will solve this?" His voice turned sharp, cutting through the tension. "Maybe we could focus on finding evidence that exonerates me, rather than putting the weight of this around Julia's neck."

"I'm working every angle." Mitchell tossed his legal pad aside before he leaned forward, concern flashing in his eyes. "Grant, I've seen you handle crises, but this one is personal. I need to know you're holding up okay."

"I'm perfectly fine," Grant muttered as he retrieved his drink. "If I lose this, it's only my entire life's work, and everything I've built goes up in smoke."

"There's no denying the pressure. But I'm concerned about your state of mind in terms of making decisions."

Grant scoffed at him before he sobered. "You're serious. What are you on the board's side now?"

"No," Mitchell said, with a shake of his head. "In business, there's nobody better. On a personal level, your judgment may not be the best."

"What's that supposed to mean?"

"It means you have an ace in the hole, but you're tying my hands. Let me use Julia."

Use Julia. The words echoed in his mind as his stomach turned over again.

"I said I'd think about it. Maybe we can avoid it if anyone did their job."

Mitchell downed the rest of his drink before he grabbed his legal pad. "I'll get working on things, and I'll keep you informed." He eyed him as he stood. "Think about what I said."

"Yeah," Grant muttered as the man left the room. He heaved a sigh, flicking his gaze to the setting sun casting long shadows across the lawn that stretched toward him with dark, spindly fingers.

For a moment, he became lost in the sunset's dying light,

the colors bleeding together to create blurred lines mirroring his current predicaments. He'd seen Mitchell look grim before, but never this grim.

He twisted to stare at the folder containing the evidence against him so far, still sitting on his desk. As his eyes rose from it, he caught sight of a new addition next to his monitor. In shiny silver that sparkled against the dark wood, a framed photo of him and Julia smiling at each other.

He grabbed it, staring down at the sparkle in her eyes as she laughed at his joke. He read the raw emotion in his own, too. He wasn't sure what scared him more: his murder trial, or the growing attraction he felt to Julia.

Their earlier conversation pushed into his brain, demanding his attention. He'd pulled away from her when the moment became too real. He couldn't let himself fall for a woman who didn't want him. She was here for a role.

"I've never met someone so genuine," Mitchell's words echoed.

Were her words and actions earlier genuine, too? He recalled the first time he'd heard her laugh, a sound so warm, it felt like home. Was there more to them than just a contract?

A knock sounded at the door, interrupting his thoughts. He called out, and Worthington stepped inside. "How did things go with Mr Caldwell?"

"Don't ask," Grant said, sinking his head into his palm, his other hand still clutching the photo.

"I take it the news is not good."

Grant gave a shake of his head, tossing the picture onto the desk.

Worthington's lips curled up at the corners as he strode forward and lifted the frame before replacing it next to the monitor. "A lovely photo of the two of you."

Grant stared at it with mixed emotions. If only he could believe it was as genuine as it appeared. He tapped the polished desk. "Can I ask you a question, Worthington?"

The man raised his chin, clasping his hands in front of him. "Certainly, sir."

"Mitch wants to put Julia on the stand as a character witness. What do you think about that?"

Worthington raised his eyebrows as he mulled it over. "It's likely a very safe bet that she'd be an excellent witness."

Grant reclined back in the chair. "Really?"

Worthington shot him a surprised glance. "You don't believe she would be?"

"It's less about her performance, and more about the request itself. It's...a lot to ask."

Worthington retrieved Grant's glass and refilled it before returning it to him. "Yes, it is. But I cannot imagine she would balk. She seems most eager to help."

Grant sipped the drink. Why was she so eager?

"Might I suggest that you speak directly to Mrs. Harrington about this? I think you may find it will alleviate any tension."

Grant clenched his fist. "I'm afraid if I bring it up to her, she'll agree."

"And that's a problem?"

Grant paused as he pictured her on the stand, being asked her motives for their marriage, hounded by the DA looking to make a name for himself.

"It's not fair to ask her to do that."

"Isn't that decision hers to make, sir?"

Grant flicked his gaze up to his butler, reading his face. "You said she'd have tension."

Worthington cracked a slight smile. "I meant it may alleviate tension on your part. I don't see much tension in Mrs.

Harrington when it comes to helping." He paused a knowing look in his eyes. "What holds you back?"

Grant's eyes lingered on the photo of them on his desk. He reached forward to trace the outline of her smiling face, the weight of the choice pressing down on him. "Guilt. She didn't expect any of this."

"None of us did. You didn't foresee a murder charge and withhold it from her."

"No, but…" A smile curled his lips, a rare moment of levity in the dark situation. "Did you know she said no to me at first?"

Worthington offered him an amused chuckle. "But you… wooed her?"

"I convinced her. Wooing is quite another matter. I'm not really certain I'd even know how to begin wooing Julia."

"I imagine it isn't that different from wooing most women."

Grant wagged a finger at him. "That is where you are wrong, Worthington. Julia is very different from most women."

"She is a most welcome change in the household, sir. I can tell you that."

"I'm glad you like her. She's only been here a few days, and I can already tell it'll be hard when she leaves."

"Perhaps it's best not to jump that far ahead, sir."

Grant's grin dissipated quickly, replaced with a grimace. "You're right. I may be in prison then."

"Let's hope not." Worthington let the statement hang for a minute. "Will you be dining in the dining room with Mrs. Harrington tonight?"

Grant heaved a sigh, wishing the answer was easier. "Yes, I think I'd better. I don't want to leave her with Sierra."

"Miss Sierra is out for the evening," Worthington answered.

"That's typical." Nothing kept Sierra from a good time. Not even a looming murder charge. Grant pulled himself from the chair. "Well, I don't want to leave her to dine alone."

"I'm certain she will appreciate that, sir. And perhaps you will find the meal enlightening."

He shook his head at his butler as he followed him from the room. While usually correct, the man was way off base this time.

Julia made her way down the stairs as he stepped out of his office. "Hi," she said in her usual soft voice. "How did it go with Mitchell?"

"Not great." They followed Worthington to the dining room.

"So, there's no chance they're dropping the charges?"

He heaved a sigh, hating to admit to her that he was in even more trouble. "No."

She remained quiet, though he couldn't tell if she was lamenting the trouble she'd strapped herself to, or something else. She chewed her lower lip for a moment, her eyebrows knitted before she opened her mouth, but he interrupted her.

"Let's not talk about it over dinner," Grant suggested.

She offered him a demure smile and nod. "Of course."

They took their seats at the table, and Worthington poured them each a glass of wine.

"So, how is your novel coming along?" Grant asked, pushing his voice to sound more enthusiastic than he felt.

"Oh, umm, it's coming," she answered, flicking her gaze down into the red wine.

He started to ask more when his phone rang. "I'm sorry." He glanced at the screen. "It's Mitchell, I need to–"

"Take it," she encouraged. "Good luck."

He rose from the table, dumping his napkin at his place, and hurried from the room, pressing the phone to his ear. "Tell me something good."

"No can do, Grant. I hate to be the bearer of more bad news, but...we've got even more trouble."

Grant's eyes slid closed as the tension built in him. Could he take more bad news?

CHAPTER 18

JULIA

*J*ulia chewed her lower lip, a storm of questions raging in her mind. She'd started to build the puzzle, but she was still missing pieces.

What am I missing?

Her mind whirled as it searched for possibilities. Who would be bold enough to kill a woman? In the high-stakes world where millions of dollars followed every deal, it could be anyone.

She stared down at her notes from the conversation with her law-enforcement-inclined sister and circled the words "crooked cop" and "DA in someone's pocket."

She shoved the paper aside and swished her mouse on the desk to wake the computer. With a search engine pulled up, she searched for the district attorney in New Orleans.

With his name in hand, she ran another search on the man, learning he was up for re-election. She sat back in her chair, tracing the edge of her pen as she considered it.

Putting someone like Grant Harrington behind bars would likely bolster his campaign. Did he owe someone a favor?

She leaned forward again, her fingers hesitating. Was she doing this to satisfy her own curiosity, or for Grant? She decided it didn't matter and clacked across the keys to find information on his donors.

As she scrolled through the online campaign finance report, detailing millions of dollars, a shiver ran down her spine, reminding her of the high-stakes world she now lived in.

A knock pulled her from her work. Worthington made his way into the room. "I've just come to collect your tea cup and inform you that dinner will be ready in twenty minutes."

"Oh, okay," she replied, a flush warming her cheeks. She caught Worthington's gaze on her screen. Was that relief and pride on his face she spotted, or was he mentally logging a list of her sins? "Is there any word on what happened with the DA meeting?"

"Not yet. Mr. Caldwell just departed. I will be checking with Mr. Harrington in a moment."

Julia nodded. "If Grant's not up to dinner…"

"I will check with him on that front, too. If not, I will–"

"I'll be down. There's no need to fuss to bring me a tray. I can eat with Sierra."

"It is no fuss at all. Miss Sierra is out."

Julia offered him a kind smile. "There is enough turmoil in this house right now that you don't need to be fretting over me. I'll come down, even if Sierra isn't here."

"If you prefer it." He flicked his gaze to the screen again, curling the corners of his lips before he disappeared.

Julia blew out a long breath as she returned her gaze to the long list of contributors. She'd need to download this and sort it to focus on the donors with a serious stake. It wouldn't be the people who donated small amounts.

She'd then have to cross-reference the large donors with anyone who may have crossed paths with Grant, particularly in business. She'd have her work cut out for her, but at least she'd be doing something useful. She didn't see how else she could help.

She clicked to download the list to tackle after her meal. Connecting the dots between campaign donors and business adversaries seemed like a long shot, but even the most unlikely connections could be revealing.

Leaving the computer behind, she rose and made her way through the halls. They seemed so quiet tonight. A pall hung over the entire house.

She couldn't imagine the pressure Grant faced. He'd already been at his wit's end with the board's pushback, and now this. She plodded down the stairs as he emerged from his office, with Worthington preceding him.

The tension in his jaw belied the weight on his shoulders.

"Hi," she said, sounding more unsure than she'd hoped. "How did it go with Mitchell?"

His face turned to stone. "Not great."

"So, there's no chance they're dropping the charges?"

The sigh he heaved made her regret asking. He probably hadn't expected to have to entertain his new fake wife while a crisis loomed.

"No."

She bit her bottom lip, her features pinching as she struggled to come up with her next statement. She wanted to tell him about her work so far, but she wasn't certain it would be appreciated.

She opened her mouth to ask about evidence when he cut her off. "Let's not talk about it over dinner."

She had her answer and plastered a smile on her face. "Of course."

They took their seats at the table. Julia fidgeted in hers as Worthington poured their wine. Maybe she should have taken Worthington up on having her dinner delivered to her. Grant seemed distracted. She wondered how much he resented her appearance for dinner.

"So, how is your novel coming?" His voice changed as though he donned a new mask of polite host.

She wouldn't blabber on and on about the topic that she was certain didn't interest him, particularly now. "Oh, umm, it's coming."

He started to answer when his phone rang. The tension built again in his face as she glanced at the screen. "I'm sorry. It's Mitchell, I need to–"

"Take it," she encouraged, adding, "Good luck."

He rose from the table, leaving her alone in the dining room. His voice echoed as he stepped from the room.

She drummed her fingers on the table, gnawing at her lower lip again.

Worthington flitted back into the room, fixing his eyes on the empty seat at the head of the long table. "I see we've lost a key member."

"Mitchell called," Julia answered as he held the plates.

"I see. Would you like your dinner now, or shall I keep it warm, along with Mr. Harrington's?"

"Uh," Julia let her eyes sink to the white tablecloth, her features pinching. "I...don't know." She slid her eyes closed, certain the butler wished she'd stop being so indecisive. She flicked her gaze to him. "I'm so sorry, Worthington."

The man set the plates aside and eased into the seat next to her. "There is nothing to apologize for. You seem...upset. Was it the call?"

She shook her head. "I'm just really not certain if

Grant would prefer me to eat alone or not. I don't want to take up his time, but I don't want to abandon him either."

The kindly butler's features softened as he took her hand in his. "I am certain he would love your company, if you don't mind waiting."

Julia swallowed hard as she nodded. "I don't. Please keep the plates warm."

"Of course, Mrs. Harrington. And please do not ever feel you are unwelcome."

Her eyebrows knit at the statement. The man was aware of their arrangement, why did he act as though they were a real married couple? Perhaps to pass off the relationship as real to any prying eyes and ears.

"Oh, Worthington," she called, her voice a mix of gratitude and curiosity.

"Yes, ma'am?"

"Is there any word on the evidence they have? Grant didn't want to talk about it, but I'm interested to know what's propelling these charges."

"I believe there is a report from Mr. Caldwell in Mr. Harrington's office. I have not seen it, though I imagine it contains the information you're interested in."

The man turned to take their plates back to the kitchen, leaving Julia alone in the room. Grant's voice carried from the nearby living room, sounding tense.

She wavered about acting on the information Worthington had given her. She probably shouldn't let herself into Grant's private office. She had no business being in there.

His heated voice barked something unintelligible in the other room.

One look couldn't hurt. She wouldn't be rifling through his private things. Perhaps she could answer some of the questions she'd discussed with her sister earlier, specifically about the amount of blood.

With her heart pounding, she tossed her napkin on her chair and scurried from the room. She power-walked her way to the foyer and glanced around before she wrapped her fingers around the cold, brass door knob.

Her stomach twisted as she pushed into the soft lighting of the richly decorated office. A single manila folder stood out starkly against the rich mahogany wood of the desk.

She crossed past the ceiling-high bookcase showcasing pictures of Grant with senators, celebrities, and even a president or two.

She reached the desk, and her breathing turned labored as blood rushed through her ears. Guilt coursed through her as she rubbed her fingers along the folder's edge. She shouldn't pry. Before she could, her eyes darted to a silver frame. The picture of her and Grant, frozen in a moment that looked like true love, beamed back at her.

She'd agreed to do this job. And she needed to know more to do it.

She flicked open the folder and scanned the information inside, including reports and photographs. She was no stranger to these. With her sister an FBI agent, and then a local cop, she'd seen her share of evidence reports, witness statements, and crime scene photographs.

She flicked to the initial report, including the transcript of the 911 call made by Evelyn's husband. The call had been initiated shortly after nine.

The claim that it had to be forty-eight hours before someone could be declared missing widely seen on television shows wasn't true, but this seemed early to log a missing persons report.

She scanned the conversation. Her husband indicated she should have been home by now and that he was worried. She wasn't answering her phone, responding to texts, or answering the office phone.

They assured him they'd send a patrol car along her route home. She flipped to the next page. It detailed the crime scene report. She scanned the notes. The car, stalled at the time of the discovery, sat near the lake. The driver's door remained open, the keys still in the ignition. Blood stains on the seat indicated an assault or foul play.

She dropped the folder on the desk as she sank into the seat and shuffled through some of the other reports. She spotted a few witness statements, along with text logs. She needed to see all of that, but right now she wanted to see the blood at the crime scene.

According to her sister, this should be a bloody crime scene.

She prepared herself for the disturbing photos as she slid to the pictures. The leather creaked under her as she tensed, ready for a scene that would haunt her nightmares.

The first photo showed the car from afar. The front door stood open, an eerie testament to the woman who had once occupied it and vanished without a trace.

Julia studied the way the car sat near the lake. It had driven over the curb, over the grass, and stopped just short of the lake, under a large maple tree.

Julia's brows knitted as she studied the photo. She traced the car's path to the lake with her finger. "This makes no sense. Why here?" The image contracted the narrative of a sudden murder, igniting a flicker of doubt in her mind.

Nothing added up. She became more convinced these charges were bogus. She'd find out in the next photo or so. There had to be an interior shot of the blood.

She sucked in a deep breath as she flicked to the next picture. It showed the well-lit interior of the silver BMW. The white leather driver's seat had a spot of blood that, according to the tape measure held to it in the photograph, was about five inches across. A few other droplets of blood stained the seat, too.

Julia bent over the picture, scouring it. Where was the blood that led them to the conclusion that she'd died from blood loss? There should be more than this.

"The bloodiest crime scene you've ever seen," her sister had said.

This couldn't possibly be enough for the charge. Something was very wrong here. She shuffled through the other photographs, finding no more evidence of blood. Nothing in the passenger seat, back seat, or trunk.

She leaned back in the seat with her brows furrowed, the photographs still splayed against the mahogany wood, and chewed her lower lip.

Her heart stopped a moment later when a voice shattered the silence. "Julia!" Grant's voice was filled with disbelief and shock.

She had been so lost in thought, she hadn't heard the footsteps approaching or creak of the door. She snapped her gaze to the ajar door, her blood going cold. Grant paused there, his usually composed features momentarily slipping as he stared at her in his chair. A glimpse of something like concern flashed through his eyes.

She leapt from his chair, the pictures fluttering to the floor.

He rushed toward her, collecting them as she bent to do the same. His hands trembled slightly as he gathered them, a small sign of his turmoil in an otherwise controlled man. The air between them was heavy and tense, a current of unsaid words and fears.

"You shouldn't be looking at these," he said, his voice low, masking a tremor of vulnerability.

"I'm sorry, I just was curious. I had to know if my suspicions were correct." Her words tumbled out in a waterfall of anxiety.

Grant's eyes, stormy with a mix of confusion, and perhaps betrayal, met hers as he snatched the photos from her. She spotted a flicker of hurt.

He ran a hand through his hair, a gesture that belied his inner turmoil. "Julia, I..." His voice faltered. "I thought you believed me?"

"I did. I do," she stammered, her heart still pounding frantically.

His brow furrowed as he snapped his gaze to her, his jaw clenched, though he did not appear angry. "What suspicions?"

"About what's really going on here. Grant, none of this adds up. I think you're being set up."

CHAPTER 19

GRANT

*G*rant eased onto the couch as he ended the phone call with Mitchell. His fingers tightened around the device until they whitened. If he didn't cling to his phone like a lifeline, he'd have whipped it across the room.

How has my life spiraled into this nightmare?

Mitchell's words echoed in his mind. "They're moving forward with the first-degree charge, in light of their latest evidence."

"Which is?"

"They found a body in the lake."

The words hung heavy in the air as Grant stopped his frantic pacing. He slid his eyes closed as the weight of emotion overcame him. He'd been hoping somehow she was still alive, but this smothered that dream.

"They're going to bring you in for more questioning. I don't know when. And the board's called an emergency meeting. They want to vote no confidence now, to remove you in light of this scandal."

"When?" His voice was hoarse with emotion.

"Two days. We may get a preliminary hearing in before then. They're out for blood, Grant."

"Seems everyone is these days," he said, with a wry smile hiding his inner turmoil.

"You know I have your back, but this is getting messier by the minute. I had hoped for better news, but..."

Grant hesitated for a moment as a question swam in his mind. He wasn't certain he wanted the answer to it, but he needed to know.

"Did they say how she...died?"

"Preliminary look by the coroner at the scene said she'd had her skull bashed in multiple times."

Silence stretched between them again before Mitchell finally spoke again. "I hate to bring this up, but unless they find something that leads them to another suspect, we're really going to need to establish you as someone who wouldn't do this. We need Julia to do that."

Grant heaved a sigh, the idea unsettling. His world continued to crumble around him, each new revelation chipping away at a new brick in his life.

And it seemed the only person who could lend him any solid ground was the person who knew him the least. That worried him. When would she turn on him? Past experience had taught him when the going got tough, his wives ran out. Would this one be any different?

"I'll think about it."

Mitchell paused for a moment before he responded. "All right. I'll start putting together our case. If they move on the new charges, call me immediately."

"I will."

He'd hung up and sat in stunned silence, replaying the

conversation over and over as his nerves continued to fray. He'd been no stranger to adversity, but this was something he never expected to face.

"We need Julia," Mitchell's voice echoed.

An image of the woman formed in his mind. He'd left her at the dinner table alone. He rose, his feet slow as he intended to return to the dining room and a meal he no longer could stomach. His gaze inadvertently fell on the massive wedding picture Sierra had hung on the wall.

A larger-than-life testament to the pack of lies his life had become, he stared at the happy smile on both their faces. If she'd only known what the first week of her marriage would bring, she would have stuck with her first answer to him when she'd fled from the nightclub. The moment of unexpected connection danced across his mind.

He couldn't return to the dining room now. He needed a moment to collect himself. He'd go to his office first. Maybe by the time he finished brooding, she'd be back in her room, and he wouldn't have to face her with the news that things somehow had managed to go from bad to worse.

He slid his phone into his pocket as he strode toward the foyer, skirting between the sweeping pair of staircases leading upstairs. He stopped when he spotted the door to his office open. He hadn't left it open.

Was Worthington inside? Odd, if Julia was still dining that he would have left her alone, but possible. He crossed the marble floor and peered in through the open door, his heart stopping.

Julia sat in his chair, with the police report open and scattered across the desk. She stared down at pictures of the crime scene. Her delicate features pinched as she studied the gruesome photos.

"Julia!" he said, his voice, filled with shock and tension, sounding harsher than he'd intended.

She snapped her gaze up at him, her eyes wide with panic. Was it fear he saw flicker through them as she spotted him? She leapt from the chair, the pictures slapping against the hardwood below her.

He rushed toward them, scooping them away from her as she joined him, collecting a few, too. "You shouldn't be looking at these," he said, desperate to control his voice.

"I'm sorry, I was just curious. I had to know if my suspicions were correct."

He raised his gaze to hers as he pulled the photos away from her. He couldn't read her face. Was she turning on him? Had she finally had enough?

He stuffed the images back into the folder before raking a hand through his hair. "Julia, I..." He swallowed hard when he couldn't find the words, struggling to keep his deluge of emotions at bay. He reined them in, making one simple statement. "I thought you believed me?"

Her features pinched. "I did. I do."

She answered quickly and easily. Then what suspicions did she have? Grant knitted his brows, his jaw tightening as he failed to read her. "What suspicions?"

"About what's really going on here. Grant, none of this adds up. I think you're being set up."

His mind reeled at the words. Had she been reading the police report to find some clue to support her idea that he'd been set up? At least she believed him, though he was about to smash her theory to bits.

He was rarely stunned into silence, but he found himself unable to force any words from his mouth to explain that the tiny boat they navigated in had sprung another leak.

She slid the folder from his hands and flicked it open. "The car, for example, why is it where it is? Why would you take her car to this location and leave it there? And why aren't there prints? If this is second-degree murder–"

"First," he answered. "They're going for first."

She froze, her eyebrows knitting together again. He dared not look at her face to see the flicker of doubt and disappointment that undoubtedly shadowed it now. "Then…"

She hesitated, and he waited for the standard betrayal to follow.

"That makes even less sense," she finished. "Now, I'm convinced this is a setup."

He slowly slid his gaze to her. He'd yet to give her the worst piece of news. The one that would shatter everything she was desperately trying to cling to.

"There's more."

She flicked her gaze to him, waiting expectantly.

"They found the body."

Her eyes fell to the folder. He imagined the hurt flashing through them as she came to the realization that things looked grim for him.

"Oh, Grant…" She heaved a sigh as she tightened her grip on the folder and slowly closed it.

He braced himself for her to leave. Maybe for good. Sierra would pitch a fit and demand she stay, as per the contract. Even if she did, he'd be in prison. His divorce papers would arrive while he sat in a cell.

"I'm so sorry. This must be so difficult. But the body turning up is hardly unexpected, right?" Her voice softened with the last statement.

"What do you mean?"

"I mean *someone* killed her. But whoever did it, I think did it so they could set you up for this murder."

His eyebrows pinched as he followed her logic, made all the more difficult by his inability to understand her support. Had she taken her contract so seriously that even this didn't rattle her? Perhaps it was easier since she was emotionally removed from this.

She flicked the folder open again before she snapped it shut. "I'm sorry if this is too difficult. I can just work out the details on my own."

"No, wait," he said as she took a step to the door. "I just... I'm sorry, I'm not following your logic."

She pulled the folder open again before shooting him a concerned glance. "Well, okay..." Julia grabbed hold of the pendant around her neck before her words tumbled from her lips. "If they're going for first-degree murder, that implies premeditation. But this..." She grabbed the photo of the car near the lake and waved it. "The car, it's abandoned, driver's door still open. It looks hasty, unplanned."

"Interrupted," he said, with a shrug. "They can make the case I was interrupted and fled the scene."

"On foot? And made it back to the office to drive home in that short of a time frame? Why would you have taken her car to begin with?" She shifted her weight again before she flipped to another picture showing a blood-stained front seat. "And this...*this* was enough to prompt a murder charge with no body?"

"There's clearly blood."

"Just here, one small spot, nowhere else in the car. Why is there blood in the driver's seat and nowhere else? Also..." She pressed her lips together before she spoke again. "This is hardly enough blood to declare someone dead."

He mulled the information. For the first time in this debacle, hope shined through. At least she believed him. Though what if she was wrong?

"I don't know the specifics of how they make that decision."

"I do. This isn't enough blood."

He furrowed his brow. She seemed confident, not only about the last part, but the entire thing. For the first time in his life, he struggled to keep up, a mix of surprise, intrigue, and awe for the woman he'd married.

"Are you sure?"

"Positive. My sister's a cop. And before she left the FBI, she worked in violent crimes for years. I've seen plenty of crime scene photos–don't tell anyone that." She shot him a pleading glance that brought a smile to his lips before she continued. "This is mild. It's hardly evidence to presume murder as a foregone conclusion."

She held the photo out in front of her as she studied it before she let it drop to her side and focused on him, her gaze probing for his take on her theory.

"Julia, I–I don't know what to say."

Her shoulders slumped slightly. "You don't agree."

"No. I..." She made several valid points. He just didn't know what to say about why she'd done it or how grateful he was that she'd shared it with him. "What you're saying makes sense, because I know I didn't do this. Someone else did this, but they seem determined to pin it on me."

She bobbed her head up and down, matter-of-factly. "A set-up. I'm certain someone benefits from this. A business rival, a member of the board who hopes to oust you?"

He clenched his jaw again as she brought up the board. "Speaking of, they've called an emergency meeting to move forward with a vote of no confidence."

Julia chewed her lower lip. He imagined her concern. Perhaps he shouldn't have been that candid with her, but something about her made it easy to open up. The way things were moving, their contract would be bust in a matter of weeks. She'd never get paid, despite her best efforts to fulfill her end of the bargain.

"We should start there first, then," she finally said. "There has to be some way we can tie together the DA with someone who's fueling this. My best guess would be campaign funds.

As a member of public office, he couldn't accept big gifts from anyone, but his campaign could."

"We'd need a list of his donors, to see if any names match up."

"I have it upstairs," she answered. "I haven't had a chance to study it yet."

His eyebrows shot up as he shot her an impressed glance. His other wives wouldn't have been nearly this resourceful.

"Wow, Julia, I am impressed."

"Don't be. This means nothing unless we can prove it in court."

It hardly meant nothing, at least not to him. She shuffled through the papers another time, her forehead pinching again.

"What are you looking for?" he asked.

"Fingerprint analysis. If you drove her car to dump the body, your prints would be there unless you wore gloves. Or wiped the car down, but then no one's prints would be here." She frowned before she flicked the folder closed with a sigh. "It's not in there, which is just another reason to think this was a hastily put-together case designed to attack your image."

He grinned at her, his familiar confidence returning for a minute. "But I have you to protect my image."

She chuckled at him. "I don't care how wholesome Sierra thinks I look on camera, I can't protect you from a murder charge without some proof."

He studied her for a moment, recalling that instant connection he'd felt with her when they'd met. "Well, I suppose I should look at that donor's list."

"Yes. We can look at it now. I downloaded it, but I haven't dug into it yet."

Grant nodded at her as he slid his arm around her shoulders and guided her to the foyer. "I'll have Worthington send dinner upstairs."

He hesitated, wondering if she wouldn't prefer that. Perhaps he'd overstepped in assuming, but she didn't seem to mind.

His mind cut to pondering their next steps, his former analytical edge returning with his newfound ally. The evening took on a more tranquil ease after the earlier turmoil, but it was soon shattered by the sudden ring of the doorbell.

Worthington whisked his way past them, his eyes lingering on Grant's hand on Julia's shoulder before he shot his employer a knowing glance. Worthington had told him a conversation with Julia would alleviate tension on his part. As usual, the man was right.

He swept the doors open as they mounted the stairs.

A strong voice announced, "New Orleans PD. We're here for Grant Harrington. Is Mr. Harrington at home?"

Grant let his eyes slide closed as he shook his head.

Julia squeezed his arm, offering him a consoling glance. "I'll call Mitchell. Do you want me to follow you?"

"No," he said, with a shake of his head. "I do not want you spending another night in that waiting room. We'll talk when I get home."

"Grant Harrington, you are under arrest for the murder of–"

"Yeah, yeah, let's just get this over with." Grant thrust his wrists forward.

The arrest was unpleasant, as was the new charge. And despite its potential to ruin his life, he went into this storm with a slight beam of light. He glanced back at it as they hauled him from the house. Could Julia save him?

CHAPTER 20

JULIA

*J*ulia's heart sank, a sense of helplessness washing over her as the cold, metallic handcuffs clasped around Grant's wrists. She bit hard into her lower lip, trying to anchor herself.

What sort of world had she gotten herself into? She'd seen so many crime scenes from her sister's work. She never thought she'd be plunged into a world of them, too.

"Mrs. Harrington?" Worthington's voice was tinged with more than just formal concern. Personal worry edged it, hitting at the loyalty to the family he'd served for years.

"Sorry," she murmured, her gaze lingering on the blue and red lights fading into the distance as the police cruiser disappeared down the long drive.

He raised a phone to her. "I have already put the call through to Mr. Caldwell. He would like to speak with you."

Julia nodded as she accepted the phone. "Hi, Mitchell, Grant's been arrested again."

"I'm on my way to the police station now. With the new charge, things are looking grim for bail, but I'll keep you informed."

"Thanks," she said, expecting the call to be over.

"Uh, Julia, did Grant happen to mention testifying on his behalf to you?"

Julia's eyebrows knitted. "No."

Mitchell sighed on the other side of the line. "He doesn't seem keen on the idea, but I'm going to be honest and say we may need you. We'll be facing a tough crowd. Someone who could…I don't know, show Grant in a more favorable light may turn the tides. But it's your call."

Julia hesitated. Could she paint a favorable picture of a man she'd only known for such a short time? She believed him, of course, but did she really know him? She'd do what she could.

"Of course, Mitchell. I'll do whatever you need. You can count on me."

"Thanks, Julia." The line disconnected, and Julia lowered the receiver, holding it out to Worthington.

"He's not sure Grant will get bail this time." Julia's mind raced with the next steps. How much could she do without Grant? She wouldn't recognize names like he would.

"How distressing," Worthington said. "Though we all appreciate your help, as I'm certain Mr. Harrington does."

She offered him a tight-lipped smile. Her help wouldn't do much good without some concrete proof. How could she get it?

"Would you like me to send your dinner up to your room?"

She sighed. "I suppose so, though I've lost my appetite."

"You should try to eat."

She nodded, with a sigh. She'd use the time to look at the list and see if she could glean any information. Maybe

197

they'd be able to get a running start whenever he came back.

Her eyebrows popped up as an idea occurred to her. "Worthington?"

"Yes, Mrs. Harrington?" he asked, turning back to face her.

"Are you familiar with any of the names of Grant's competitors?"

He puckered his lips, clasping his hands in front of him. "I may recognize them. Why do you ask?"

"Would you mind joining me for dinner? I have a project I'd really like your help with."

"Certainly, Mrs. Harrington. I will meet you in your office."

She smiled at him before he strode to the kitchen, and she climbed the stairs. She wondered if Sierra was home. Someone should tell her the latest developments before she heard it on the news.

Julia dug her phone out of her pocket and stared down at it. Was it her place to call Sierra?

Who else would do it if she didn't? With another moment's hesitation, she pressed the call button next to Sierra's name. The line trilled on the other side as her heart thudded against her ribs. Why, she couldn't say, but the idea of having to pass bad news to Sierra made her palms sweat.

Sierra's sharp voice answered. "Stepmommy? I hope this isn't a butt dial."

Julia tempered her sigh as she answered. "No, it isn't. I'm afraid I have some bad news."

The sarcasm melted from Sierra's voice, replaced with an undertone of genuine concern. "Is it Daddy? Is something wrong? What happened?"

A male voice sounded in the background. "Come back to bed."

Julia paused, her eyebrows knitting. The voice sounded so familiar, but she couldn't place it. Sierra hissed something before she returned her voice to full volume.

"Julia? Hello? What's wrong?"

"Your father was arrested again."

"For what now?" she shouted.

"Same thing, new charge. And they found the body. I didn't want you to see it on the news."

"They found Evelyn?" Her voice cracked, and Julia detected a hint of raw, genuine emotion.

She nodded, despite Sierra not being able to see her. "Yes. I'm sorry, Sierra. I think things are going to get a little worse before they get better."

"Did you call Mitchell?"

"He's on his way to the station."

Silence stretched between them for a few seconds before Sierra snapped, "If anything else happens, let me know." The line clicked, and Julia pulled the phone from her ear, staring down at it.

She shoved the device in her pocket as she continued to her room. It wasn't any of her business who Sierra was with. And she had more important things to piece together. But that voice in the background nagged at her. Something lingered in her mind, but she needed to focus on the immediate crisis.

It would take concentration to delve into the depths of potential culprits, searching for a clue that could turn the tide.

She stepped into her office with a sigh and shuffled to the computer, waking it as she sank into her chair.

Her phone buzzed in her pocket, and she dug for it, hoping for some news on Grant. Instead, she found a text from her sister.

How's that plot coming along?

As she waited for the donor spreadsheet to load, she typed back her answer.

Still working out the details.

Names, contributions, and a variety of other information populated the screen as her phone chimed again.

If you need anything else, just call.

She fired off a text, telling Alicia she'd reach out if she needed more information and dumped the phone on the desk before she scrolled through the list. Thousands of entries. She let her chin sink into her palm as an overwhelming feeling sped up her heart.

A second later, her phone chimed again. She glanced at the lock screen's preview, her muscles tightening again at the words. She shoved the phone aside, not willing to answer the message at the moment.

"Is there any word?" Worthington asked as he entered with a maid trailing behind him with a second tray.

"No," Julia said, with a frown. "Unfortunately not. Please sit down."

He pulled a chair closer to her desk as she pushed her food around with her fork. "Now, what is it you hope I can help with?"

Julia left the food untouched, returning her attention to the monitor. "I think Grant is being set up. There is no way any DA who is not looking to pay back a favor could have come to a murder charge as quickly as they did."

Worthington's eyebrows knitted. "I am pleased to hear you say that. Mr. Harrington is not a killer."

"I don't think so either. But without some solid proof that he's being railroaded, our belief in him isn't going to sway a jury."

"So, what are we looking for?"

Julia glanced at the spreadsheet on the screen as her mind worked to seek an avenue forward. "A donor who is a business rival or something. I don't know. We need some sort of lead. Some way to track down who may actually be responsible for this."

"I see. And what are we looking at here?"

Julia leaned in closer, scrolling through the list. "This is the donor list for the DA's latest campaign. I'd like to search it for any potential suspects. It's probably a long shot, but maybe we can find a suspect hiding in plain sight. After that…well, let's work on this first." She scrolled up and down the list again as she bit into her lower lip.

"There appear to be thousands of names here. It will take several hours to sort this out."

Julia shook her head. "No, we can narrow this down. For example, John Watkins gave one hundred dollars. I'd guess DA Donovan would not do anything questionable for that amount."

"Good thinking."

Julia tapped to filter the information. "Let's look at donations of over ten thousand dollars only. That should narrow the list considerably."

"That's an excellent idea, Mrs. Harrington."

The list populated again, removing anyone who donated less than ten thousand dollars. It produced a much smaller list.

"Okay, we've got fifty-seven donors left to look through."

Julia scanned the names before she twisted to face Worthington.

He flicked his gaze over the untouched food as the bright computer screen cast shadows over it. "You should eat. Mr. Harrington will be very displeased with me if I let you go hungry."

She accepted it and forced down a few bites. "Thank you. I'll hardly starve, though. Now, is there anyone on this list you think could have orchestrated this?"

Worthington leaned closer and scrolled through the names on the list. "I recognize several of these, though I am not certain they would have done this."

A crease formed between Julia's brows and tension built in her shoulders as they found no clear smoking gun. She'd hoped for something, anything that could lead them to a breakthrough.

"Can you highlight the names you know?"

Worthington's hand fumbled the mouse a bit. "Ah, I'm afraid…"

"It's okay, I can do it if you just tell me the names you recognized."

Worthington nodded and rattled off five names from the list.

Julia highlighted the cells of each. "Any others?"

Worthington hesitated, his fingers drumming against the desk. "No, and…to be completely honest, these are not rivals, really. I am not certain if that matters."

"Anyone from his board?"

Worthington shook his head.

Julia glanced back at the screen, chewing her lower lip.

"I'm afraid I haven't helped you at all."

She snapped her gaze to him, offering an appreciative smile. "No, you've helped me very much. I'll start tracking down information on any of these individuals, to see what I can find."

"If I can be of any further help, please ask. I have been with Mr. Harrington for many years. He does not deserve this." Worthington smiled as he rose from his chair.

"I agree with you," Julia said. "I'll do everything I can."

Worthington offered her an appreciative smile before he collected his tray and left the room. Julia took a few more bites of hers before she glanced at her phone again. She toggled it on to glance at the message before she decided to answer it later, delving into research on the names Worthington had identified.

She spent hours scouring the Internet for some hint as to why any of the highlighted names would have been involved, or some clue as to how to link them to the crime, but found nothing.

As she leaned back in her chair, biting her index thumb with a sigh, her phone jangled, buzzing across the desk's polished wood. She snatched it and answered without checking the ID, figuring it would be Mitchell with an update.

"You could just say no instead of ignoring me for hours," her sister's voice said.

Her heart skipped a beat as she recalled the ignored message from earlier. "I–I'm sorry, Ally, I got really involved in some research and didn't even see your message."

"Uh huh, right. The minute I asked about you coming home, you suddenly got busy with research."

Julia chewed her lower lip, her habit when processing information. "I told you–"

"I know, I know. You didn't see it. I'm a cop, remember? I can tell when you're lying."

"Cops aren't lie detectors."

"No, but sisters are. This is the third time you've dodged this question."

Julia slid her eyes closed as her hand instinctively went to the compass pendant around her neck, its weight a grounding reminder of choices and directions.

"I'm just–"

"Busy. I know. You said that the last time, and the time before."

Julia's mind raced. She couldn't leave now. She wondered if she could get away discreetly some time over the next year. She wasn't certain she could avoid a visit with her sister much longer. And she couldn't have her come to New Orleans.

"Umm, maybe around the holidays," she said, with a shrug.

"Do you promise?"

Julia chewed her lower lip. She couldn't promise, but the holidays may be an opportune time to allow the family some time alone.

"Yeah, I didn't think so," Alicia answered before she could.

"I'll try, Alicia. In fact, I'll check plane ticket prices later this week, to see when it would be best."

"Oh, progress. A promise to at least consider coming back to Harbor Cove."

Julia tried to chuckle, but between the latest events with Grant that seemed to be consuming her life to the memories of her hometown, to the uncertainty of her contract and the complications it was causing in her life, it came out sounding hollow.

"I promise I'll look."

"If you need money–"

"No. I don't. I just…I'll look, Alicia, okay?"

"You can't stay away forever, sis. You have to face it sometime."

Julia closed her eyes, letting the compass drop from her fingers. Flashbacks of the people she'd left behind, specifically the one who had given her the compass, made her fidget in her seat.

"I know."

"Oh, Juju, it'll be okay. Let me know what you come up with for travel plans."

"I will."

Her sister blew her a kiss through the phone and they said their goodnights before they hung up. Julia checked her phone for any other notifications, but she found nothing.

Her shoulders slumped as she dragged herself from her chair and shuffled into her bedroom. She peeled off her clothes and changed into her pajamas before sliding between the soft, silky sheets.

With a pillow hugged to her chest, she sat propped up as her mind wandered down path after path, in search of answers. She found none.

In search of a distraction, she grabbed the television remote and turned on the set. At this hour, the late-night news should be on.

She waited through the commercial before the pounding beat of the news' intro music sounded. "Breaking news tonight in the Harrington murder case," the serious blonde said.

The camera flashed off her and to pre-recorded footage of officers at the lake. "Divers have found a body they believe to be that of sixty-two-year-old Evelyn Clarke. Mrs. Clarke was missing and presumed dead two days ago. Grant Harrington, CEO of Harrington Global, has been accused of the crime."

A mugshot of her husband appeared on the screen.

"The DA called the discovery a win for the case against Harrington, applauding the hard work of the officers who dredged the river for days in search of the remains. He called it an act of God, since finding the body was like finding a needle in a haystack."

Julia snapped off the television and tossed the remote on the bed next to her. "An act of God, I'll bet. Must have been hard to find it right where your partner put it."

Her phone chimed a second later. She checked the display, finding a message from Mitchell.

No bail tonight, preliminary hearing tomorrow 9am.

She crossed her arms, tapping her foot in the air as she fumed over the charade and scoffed. "Needle in a haystack."

Her foot slowed as her mind slowly pieced together an idea. Needles were small. And in a haystack they were hidden, impossible to find. So would any wayward donations tying a crooked DA to whoever pulled his strings.

She had been wrong to search for big donors only. She needed to search for small ones. Several small donations from the same entity would add up to a large one.

Her heart skipped a beat as she threw off the covers and hurried from her bedroom to her office. She shimmied the mouse to wake the computer. The donor's list still sat there, with the filter for large donors.

She cleared it and clicked to create a table showing each donor with the number of donations. It populated on a new page. Most of the donors had the number one next to their names, some had twos. She licked her lips as she scrolled in search of anything larger.

Three-quarters of the way through the list, her heart stopped. In the midst of all the small numbers, one large one stared her in the face. "One hundred and thirty-seven contributions."

Her shaky finger hovered over the mouse, her pulse quickening. The name "DG Industries, LLC" glared from the screen.

With the original spreadsheet active, she searched for the name, finding it with several smaller amounts. She totaled them up, finding it added up to over one hundred thousand dollars.

Her lips curled on the edges as she slapped a hand against the desk. "Bingo!"

She opened a browser and spent hours trying to find any information on this company. It appeared to serve no function, and finding information was difficult. By two in the morning, all she'd cobbled together was an address.

She punched it into the map and viewed the location.

Satellite mode showed what appeared to be an abandoned warehouse. She sat back in the chair as something niggled at her. She needed to track the information, and she needed to do it quickly.

With the board vote in two days and preliminary hearing hours away, they couldn't waste time. But she needed help to do it. After hastily pulling on clothes, she hurried from her bedroom, down the stairs, and out the front door. Moonlight cast the opulent estate in haunting shadows as she hurried through the cool night air, tugging her sweater tighter around her. Each step cut through the eerie stillness of the night until she reached the house the chauffeur lived in off the massive multi-car garage.

She pounded on the door, her heart in her throat as she wondered if they'd find anything useful. A light cut through the darkness in the house, and the door opened seconds later.

James tugged a shirt on, his eyes slits. "Mrs. Harrington?"

She ran a hand through her hair, her voice hurried. "Oh, James, I'm so sorry for waking you, but I need your help."

"Is everything okay? Are you sick?"

"No, no. I'm not. I've been tracking some information on the case against Grant...I..." Julia glanced up at his pinched features as he tried to make sense of her story. "I'm sorry, I shouldn't have done this in the middle of the night."

"No, no, it's okay. Come in." He heaved out a laugh. "It's not like I can go back to bed after hearing that."

She stepped into his house, freezing at his last words. That voice.

Come back to bed.

Her eyes went wide. Sierra had been with James.

CHAPTER 21

GRANT

*G*rant drummed his fingers on the cold, metal table, the handcuffs still clinking around his wrists. The unforgiving chair pressed into his back in the suffocatingly small, starkly lit room that felt smaller by the minute.

The cop across from him slouched in the chair, his face hardened with displeasure. "We can't help you if you don't help us."

Grant heaved a sigh. "I've already told you, I am not talking without my attorney present."

"Still playing silent? Classic move from the guilty party—lawyer up, clam up. Seen it a hundred times. We can't help you unless you talk, though."

Grant resisted the urge to roll his eyes at the man. The game they were playing was one he wasn't interested in. He'd been ripped away from Harrington House at the wrong moment. He and Julia were about to try to find a path forward to determine the real culprit here.

The cop leaned forward, his voice a low growl. "You know, people like you think you can get away with anything. But not this time."

Grant's hand clenched involuntarily as a surge of annoyance turned to anger. He reminded himself to stay calm and not give in to provocation.

The man across from him gathered his papers and snapped the folder shut. "It's your funeral, Harrington."

He shuffled from the room and slammed the door shut behind him, leaving Grant alone in the cold, starkly lit space.

Grant leaned forward, cupping his forehead in his palms. His second arrest marked the second time he'd been ripped away from his new wife at the exact wrong moment. He recalled the sight of her in the sapphire blue dress as she entered the ballroom, uncertain if it rivaled the moment burned into his mind from earlier, when she'd showcased how quickly her mind moved to solve problems.

He remained lost in thought when the door burst open. A grim-faced Mitchell entered, snapping his mind back to reality.

"We really need to quit meeting under these circumstances," Grant said.

"Believe me, I'd love to." Mitchell slid into the seat and snapped open his briefcase. "You seem to be in somewhat better spirits despite the situation being worse than it was before."

"Not as good of spirits as I'll be in when you get these charges dismissed."

Mitchell uncapped his pen and scribbled on his paper. "The good news on that front is, Julia is willing to testify on your behalf."

Grant stared at his legal counsel, his features tightening. "I told you I'd think about that."

"And when you were arrested for a second time, I took it upon myself to ask your lovely new bride myself. She agreed. That's one thing that'll go our way."

Grant felt a twinge in his chest, a mix of both relief and concern. Given her adamant display in his office earlier, she likely could turn the tides for him, but at what cost? The harsh glare of the courtroom and twisted portrayals by the prosecution may prove too much for her.

"How about the fact that I didn't do this? That the evidence is all circumstantial?"

"We're not just up against circumstantial evidence anymore. With the body turning up, the DA's got a tangible narrative. We need to dismantle it, piece by piece, especially since you don't have an alibi."

Grant drummed his fingers against the table. "Do we have to answer any of their questions?"

"Maintain the Fifth, Grant. Don't give them anything to pounce on. We've cooperated as much as we're going to."

"Fine. When can you get me out of here?" His voice had its usual demanding tone.

Mitchell sucked in a sharp breath. "I'm doing the best I can, but finding a judge that'll grant you bail a second time isn't going to be easy."

Grant huffed, tightening his fist in frustration. "Mitchell. I have matters that need tending to. I can't be stuck here."

"I'm pushing for a preliminary hearing tomorrow morning. I'll make a motion to dismiss the charges based on insufficient evidence, but that's a long shot in a preliminary hearing."

Grant's mind processed the information and the timing. "What are our odds?"

"Nothing you'd find acceptable."

Grant threw himself into the chair's back, with a sigh. "I don't like this. Not with the board meeting hanging over my head. You've got to get me out of here so I can handle that."

"I'm doing my best, but this is a legal maze. This DA smells blood in the water, and he's looking for a high-profile conviction. He's risen in the polls since the announcement of your arrest. He wants to keep the momentum going."

Grant slammed his hands against the table as his frustration built. "How can this be happening?"

Mitchell raised his gaze over the rim of his reading glasses, his expression making it clear he didn't appreciate the behavior. "Those types of displays are exactly what they're going to say led to Evelyn's murder."

Grant leaned back and shook his head, his jaw clenching. "What I mean is, aren't there laws to stop being railroaded like this?"

Mitchell made a few more notes on his legal pad, keeping his eyes trained on the paper. "Yes. Let's hope the judge sees things our way."

"He'd better. I can't be locked up like this. Not if I'm going to save my company."

Mitchell bobbed his head up and down, but the arrival of two detectives prevented any further conversation.

Mitchell abandoned his seat, joining Grant on the same side of the table as the other two men sat across from them. One glanced through a folder before he passed it off to his partner.

"Anything you'd like to share with us?"

Grant glanced at Mitchell, who responded for him. "If you'd like to ask a specific question, feel free, though I can't guarantee I'd advise my client to answer it."

"Evelyn Clarke worked for Harrington Global–for you– for over twenty years."

"Is there a question in there?" Grant shot back.

"Why did you do it? Did you just snap? She bring you the wrong file and the pressure got to you? Or have you been planning this for a while?"

Grant bit his tongue before he reacted to the bait and ended up in more trouble than he already was. He just needed to stay calm and wait this out. Though with the clock ticking, he found it harder and harder to control his temper.

"All right, fine. Let's come at this another way. Tell me about your relationship with Ms. Clarke. Any recent tensions we should know about?"

"I'm advising my client not to answer that," Mitchell said.

The officer heaved a sigh as he settled into his seat. "All right. Tell us again where you were on Monday night, between the hours of nine-thirty and eleven."

After a glance at Mitchell, who offered a slight nod, Grant said, "I told you. I went home, I had dinner with my wife. I realized I'd forgotten a file. I called my chauffeur and asked for him to bring a car around. I went back to the office, I picked it up, and I went home."

"What time did you arrive home, exactly?"

"Ten-thirty."

The officer glanced at his partner before he nodded. "And you left your place around?"

"Nine-thirty."

"Which gives you ample time to commit this crime. Especially if you planned it ahead of time."

Mitchell heaved a sigh. "Gentlemen, let's keep our conjectures to ourselves, shall we? We're answering questions in good faith. We are not here for you to berate my client."

"Your client killed a loyal employee of his–"

"A fact that has not been established or admitted. Move on." Mitchell kept his eyes trained on the detectives, not flinching.

"When was the last time you and Mrs. Clarke had a disagreement?"

"I can't recall."

"Really? You keep up with a multinational corporation, and you can't remember when you and she had words?"

"No, I can't. It didn't happen often. Evie was always on top of things." Grant's voice faltered as he realized his long-time friend never would set foot in his office again. He stared at a blank spot on the wall, trying to anchor himself.

The officer flicked up his eyebrows. "Oh, I get it. When it did happen, like Monday night, you couldn't handle it."

"That's not what I said," Grant snapped, his voice a low growl.

The officer's lips curled on the edge as he narrowed his eyes. "Seems like you have a temper."

Grant tightened his lips, squeezing his fingers into fists as he silently seethed.

"Is that true?" the officer prodded.

"We're not here to assess my client's behaviors," Mitchell responded.

The officer locked eyes with Grant. "I think it is true. I'll bet if we asked your pretty little wife about that, she'd tell us she's afraid of you."

Grant lunged at the man. Mitchell burst from his seat, grabbing his shoulders as the officer kicked his chair back away from the table, an amused glance on his features.

"Whoa. That hit a nerve. Don't like people talking about the little missus, huh?"

Mitchell dropped his voice to a whisper. "Remember what we talked about. They're just trying to rattle you."

Grant's nostrils flared as he settled back into his seat, his hackles still raised from the remark.

The officer leaned forward, the look of amusement still

on his face. "I wonder if poor Evelyn Clarke said the wrong thing that night about Julia."

"Okay, I think that's enough conjecture on your part, Detective," Mitchell said, tossing his legal pad on the metal table.

"Oh, I don't think it's even close to enough, Mr. Caldwell."

"Well, I do. This interview is over. You're only attempting to needle at my client using any means you can. Mrs. Harrington has nothing to do with this matter whatsoever, but you've brought up her name multiple times. This ends now."

The man held Grant's gaze for another second before he shrugged nonchalantly. "Fine, have it your way. I'll happily escort him to a holding cell."

"I'd like another moment with him before that."

The man rose from his seat and swiped his folder off the table. "We're gonna nail you on this."

He strode from the room with his quiet partner, slamming the door behind them.

"Mitchell–"

"Don't apologize. Grant, you've got to keep yourself together better than that. That cannot happen again."

"He shouldn't have brought up Julia."

"They're going to go after anything they can that they see as a weakness. You have to control your temper. If we put Julia on the stand, I can't have you attacking the DA when he asks her if she's afraid of you."

Grant heaved a sigh. "It won't happen again, because you're not putting her on the stand."

Mitchell opened his mouth to reply before shaking his head. "We'll talk about that later. For now, keep your emotions under control. It'll make my job far easier."

Grant heaved a sigh as Mitchell rose, collected his briefcase, and strode from the room. A uniformed officer entered a moment later and hauled him to his feet. The stark fluorescent lights of the hall stung his eyes as the man led him through the halls to the holding cells.

As the bars clanked closed, he heaved a long sigh. His first thoughts went to Julia. They would rip her apart on the stand. He couldn't let that happen. He had to find a way out of this that didn't expose her to the people who were after him.

An hour passed before Mitchell returned, informing him of the preliminary hearing scheduled for first thing the following morning. He'd already texted Julia. Her show of support may help with something.

Grant settled in for a long night on the uncomfortable cot, a far cry from the thousand-count Egyptian cotton sheets on his perfectly molded bed at Harrington House. The hours passed without him getting much sleep.

Instead, he dwelled on all of the things he couldn't control, from the courtroom battle to the boardroom vote, and finally to Julia.

He'd see her soon, and he hoped they'd have the chance to talk. As the morning hour approached, Mitchell appeared at his cell, an electric shaver in hand.

"Remember what we talked about last night, Grant. No outbursts. I don't care how unfair they seem, or what hits your reputation take…" He paused, waiting to catch Grant's eyes. "What's said about Julia."

Grant heaved a sigh as he shook his head before he continued with his shaving. "That guy had it coming to him. He was out of line way before that."

"But you didn't go after him until her name came up. She's a trigger for you. Don't react."

Grant clicked off the shaver before he buttoned his top button and slipped his tie under his collar. "Fine. No outbursts. Just get these charges dismissed, or at least get me out on bail."

"I'll do my best. You do *your* best to make that easy for me."

Grant finished with his tie, adjusting it tighter around his neck before he tugged on his suit jacket. "I'll be on my best behavior."

Mitchell eyed him with an unamused glance, though the corners of his lips tugged up at Grant's new attitude as an officer unlocked the cell and slipped handcuffs around Grant's wrists.

He led them to the courtroom for their hearing. He stared at the image of Lady Justice, thinking justice was anything but blind. Mitchell took his seat, poured a glass of water, and took a sip before he reviewed his notes.

Grant stared at the clock at the back of the courtroom. Quarter-to-nine. Julia wasn't here yet. He'd been surprised not to see her waiting already. He drummed his fingers on the table as he watched the double doors in the back.

They swept open, and a reporter stepped inside, finding a seat behind the DA's table. "You said you told Julia, right?" Grant asked Mitchell.

"Mm-hmm," he said as he scrawled something on his legal pad. "Texted her last night."

"Did she answer you?"

The man slipped his phone from his pocket and checked. "No. Though I sent the text late. She may have been asleep."

With a sigh, Grant settled back in his seat, twisting to watch the door again. It opened, and his heart rose, only to find Sierra saunter through. She hurried to a seat behind him and squeezed his shoulder.

"Hi, Daddy. You look tired."

"Thanks, sweetheart. Where's Julia?"

Sierra shrugged. "How am I supposed to know?"

"Well, did you see her this morning?" Grant's heart skipped a beat.

"No. She wasn't there. I knocked, but she wasn't in her room. Worthington said she hadn't been down for breakfast."

His heart thudded faster against his ribs. "Has anyone seen her?"

Sierra arched an eyebrow as she lifted a shoulder. "I'll try calling her."

She whipped her phone from her designer bag and tapped Julia's name, placing the call on speakerphone. The line trilled several times before a recorded message played.

"Hi, you've reached Julia Stanton. I can't take your call right now, but if you leave your name and number, I'll get back to you as soon as possible. Bye!"

Grant stared in disbelief at the phone as Sierra ended the call with a click of her tongue. "I can't believe this."

"Me either," Grant said as he rubbed his chin.

"She hasn't even changed her voicemail to her new last name yet."

Grant stared at his daughter for a breath. "Not that. Where is she?"

His mind stretched to find answers. He'd thought they had been on the same page last night. He'd expected to see her this morning. His palms turned sweaty as he gripped the table while the room closed in around him.

Where is Julia?

CHAPTER 22

JULIA

*J*ulia's breath hitched, her gaze lingering on the chauffeur's retreating form. A shiver traced her spine as recognition bloomed. It had been his voice she'd heard earlier when she'd called Sierra. Her head swam as questions formed.

James twisted to face her, his features pinching. "Mrs. Harrington? Are you all right?"

She blinked rapidly, her thoughts a jumble.

"Maybe you better sit down." James gently wrapped an arm around her shoulders as he led her to a stool at the breakfast bar and eased her onto it.

She stared at two empty wine glasses on the counter in front of her, one smudged with the same shade of lipstick Sierra wore.

James perched on the seat next to her. "You said something about the case against Mr. Harrington?"

Julia ran a hand through her hair as she turned to face

him, her eyes still wide. She swallowed hard, shaking her head to clear her thoughts.

"Yes, uhh…I think Grant's being set up."

James mulled it before he nodded. "Okay. And you said you needed my help."

"Yes." She tugged a scrap of paper from her pocket and slapped it on the marbled counter. "I need to go to this address."

James studied the paper, his forehead creasing. "Why here? Why now?" His voice blended skepticism with concern.

Julia's heart hammered in her chest, a storm of anxiety swirling within her. Julia forced her mind and speech to slow as she explained.

"I've been trying to figure out who would do this. I scoured the campaign list for someone who may have done this. The only clue I found is a company called DG Industries. They made over one hundred and thirty contributions to the DA's campaign, totaling over one hundred thousand dollars."

James bobbed his head up and down. "And you think they had something to do with Mr. Harrington's arrest?"

"Yes," Julia said with a nod, twisting in her seat. "Yes, the evidence they have doesn't add up. It's like…" She paused, searching the dark flecks in the granite countertop as the first rays of morning light cast a soft glow over the kitchen. "It's all wrong. It's like they're framing him, manufacturing evidence out of thin air."

"So, what does this address have to do with it?"

"I figured whoever was doing this was funneling money into the DA's campaign. At first I looked for major donors, but I couldn't find much there. But then I looked for the most donations. I found DG Industries. This is their address."

"Okay, surely this is something better handled by Mitch Caldwell's team or Max."

Julia heaved a sigh as she fidgeted in the seat. They didn't have time. She wasn't the detective in the family, but with the hearing in only a few short hours, she had to take action. Max wouldn't be in soon enough.

She shook her head. "I just need a car to check this out."

James sucked in a breath, shaking his head. "This is a bad idea. We should leave it to the security team."

"There's no time for that. No, I'm going now."

"Okay, okay," James said, holding up a hand. "You're going to go whether I help you or not, aren't you?"

"I could call a cab if you don't," she answered.

James cracked a smile at her and shook his head. "Yeah, that's not a great part of town, and Mr. Harrington will never forgive me if something happens to you. Just let me get some clothes on. I'll take you."

He patted her shoulder as he slid off the stool and padded his way toward the stairs leading to the loft bedroom. "So, what do you think we'll find there?"

Julia drummed her fingers on the cold granite as a knot formed in her stomach. Sunlight cast a warm glow over the countertop and stainless steel appliances, though she felt anything but warm.

A mix of feelings shot through her, but despite the risks, they needed information. "I'm not sure. Maybe nothing, but…Grant's hearing is in a few hours. If there is *anything* that could help, we need to find it now."

James hurried down the stairs, a crease of worry etching his brow as he slid a clip into his handgun.

Julia's heart stopped as she spotted it, her eyes going wide.

James glanced up at her before he stowed it in his waist-band. "Just a precaution."

She forced a weak, fleeting smile onto her lips before she nodded.

James wrapped an arm around her shoulders and guided her to a door at the back of the kitchen. After flinging it open and shuffling her inside, he flicked on the lights. Row after row of fluorescents hummed to life in the oversized garage.

Julia's jaw dropped open as she swept her gaze over the more than twenty vehicles in the garage.

James flicked open a box filled with keys. "Take your pick."

"He has this many cars?"

James shrugged as he grabbed a set of keys and led Julia to a small BMW SUV. He opened the back door, but she bypassed him.

"I'll ride shotgun, thanks."

She tugged the door open and climbed inside as James circled around and slid in behind the driver's seat. "I am never going to hear the end of this."

Julia grinned at him as the engine roared to life and the garage door slid open. The bright morning sun beamed down as they pulled down the drive.

James palmed his cell phone and tapped a few times before he pressed the phone to his ear. "Max, when you get this, send a couple of guys to Four-five-two-three Harbinger, in the Weston Industrial Park."

Julia studied him for a moment before she returned her gaze to the street spreading in front of her, bathed in the bright morning sunlight. She checked the time, her fingers tightening around her phone as each minute ticked past.

They slowed as they hit a snarl of traffic. Julia let her head thud back against the headrest. "Come on."

James shot her a sideways glance as he inched forward. "So, how did you find this information?"

"Oh, umm, well if you look at the facts, nothing adds up.

So, I figured this must be a setup. The only way this works, though, is if the DA goes along with it. Honestly, he should know better than to have set up the charges he did. So, I dug into his campaign list."

"And DG Industries is a donor?"

"Yes. Mostly small donations, but they made so many, it added up to a big contribution."

James rubbed at the stubble on his face as he considered it. "Who owns it?"

"I couldn't find that information. Just this address. It's a long shot, but I can't just do nothing."

James sped up as the light changed. "Mr. Harrington really got lucky when he married you."

Julia bit into her lower lip, uncertain of how to answer. She decided on an awkward smile at him before she returned to drumming her fingers against the door handle.

"Not much longer," he promised.

The eighteen minutes showing on the GPS screen ticked by far too slowly for Julia's taste. She raked her sweaty palms against her pants as her heart thudded. Her eyes flicked to the courthouse rising in the distance. Everything would unfold there in a matter of hours. Would they find anything to help?

They finally swung onto Harbinger Street. Julia glanced up at the string of abandoned buildings decorated with colorful graffiti and broken windows. Julia's heart pounded in her ears as they neared the address. The leather of the car seat felt cold against her skin, heightening her sense of unease.

Her hope waned. They'd likely find only an empty warehouse, a shell listed on the paperwork to hide the truth about the company.

James slowed the car to a stop, throwing the gear shifter into park. "I'll check it out first–"

"No," Julia said with a shake of her head as she swung the door open and slid out of the car.

James sucked in a breath. "You are bound and determined to get me on Mr. Harrington's bad side."

"If we find something here that gets the charges against him dismissed, I think he'll owe you."

"I'm going to let you manage that," James said as they studied the red brick exterior.

The warehouse loomed before them, its large facade standing strong. Shadows danced across the broken windows, and a chill ran down Julia's spine.

She crossed to a metal door, scratched and dented. She tugged on it, but it didn't budge. A curse escaped her as James joined her.

"I'll head around back and see if—"

He stopped, his eyes going wide as she pulled a lock pick kit from her pocket.

Julia's cheeks burned as she shot a glance his way. "Don't judge."

He held his hands up as she slid it into the lock and easily opened it. James hurried through the door and pushed Julia behind him.

"Stay back."

They crept forward, the air musty and thick with dust. Each step echoed in the cavernous space, shadows stretching like long fingers from the dim light filtering through the filthy windows.

Julia peered around James's tall, bulky form, her heart sinking with every step. The warehouse looked empty. Perhaps they'd find nothing here.

"There's an office upstairs," James said, poking his finger at a loft suspended over the floor. "Maybe there's something up there."

"You check it out. I'll finish the sweep down here."

"Mrs. Harrington…" James cocked his head as he began to shake it.

"The place looks abandoned, James. This is probably hopeless."

He heaved a sigh but nodded. "Yell if you find anything."

"You do the same."

With a nod, James trotted forward and climbed the stairs toward the office, while Julia spun in search of anything on the ground floor. Her stomach twisted into a knot as she found nothing but dust, dirt, and grime.

She shuffled through the dust-mote-filled air toward a dark corner. A rat scurried out, squealing as it raced past her.

She shuddered and grimaced as she dashed in the opposite direction and into a back hall. Wrapping her arms around her midriff, she wandered through the back storage rooms.

"Come on," she whispered, her voice lost in the vast emptiness of the warehouse. Shadows closed in around her, mirroring the sinking feeling in her chest. Maybe James had had more luck upstairs. They just needed a name or something to point to who may be behind this.

She checked her phone. Nearly nine. She'd be late for his hearing. She was a fool for coming here. Not only would this not pan out, Grant would face the courtroom alone.

So much for her improving his image. She'd fail at her first major task.

Julia slid her eyes closed as tears burned them. Exhaustion from her sleepless night was catching up with her. She opened her eyes, blinking away her emotions before she pressed on.

She glanced into two more boxy rooms before she continued toward a set of hanging plastic curtains.

She shoved them aside, a sticky grease coating her hand as she slid through into another room. Her breath caught in her throat as she stepped into the dimly lit space. In the center, something–or someone–that defied belief. Her hand flew to her mouth, her eyes wide with shock and disbelief.

"Oh, my word!"

Julia's knees wobbled as her mind struggled to process the information in front of her. How could this be?

There, amidst the shadows, sat Evelyn Clarke, a fragile figure bound to a metal chair, her eyes wide with fear. Duct tape was plastered over her mouth, silencing her cries. Julia's heart tightened in disbelief. Against all odds, Evelyn was very much alive.

"Evelyn!" Julia exclaimed as she rushed forward and dropped to her knees. "You're alive."

She murmured something unintelligible, her tear-stained cheeks tugging against the tape.

"It's okay. Let me get this tape off your mouth." Julia carefully tried to peel the corner away from her lips, trying to be gentle with the woman's delicate skin.

Evelyn gasped as Julia yanked the tape away before her eyes fell over Julia's shoulder and went wide. "Look out!"

Suddenly, a shadow loomed behind her. Julia's heart leapt. She barely registered the movement before a crushing blow slammed into her skull. Pain exploded in her head, stars dancing before her eyes as she stumbled, disoriented and reeling from the impact.

She pressed a hand to her head as warm liquid slid through her hairline. When she pulled her fingers away, she found them tinged in blood.

Her vision swam as she glanced up at her attacker. A masked man wielded a bat and strode toward her, his heavy boots echoing in her head. Despite the screaming pain, she stumbled backward, ramming into a wall behind her.

Julia gasped, each breath a battle. The room spun, the

attacker's silhouette blurring and sharpening as her eyes struggled to focus.

She prepared for another blow. As the attacker advanced, a cold realization washed over her. She may have found Evelyn alive, but now they were both trapped. Their fate hung by a thread. A tear ran down her cheek as she desperately searched for a solution.

CHAPTER 23

G RANT

Grant felt his chest constrict, each breath a battle. He pressed his clammy hands against the cool, polished wood before reaching for the water to quench his parched throat. The bailiff shuffled into the courtroom and ordered them to rise for the judge's entrance. He rose, his eyes trained on the grain of the wooden table in front of him.

Why is Julia not here? Has she changed her mind?

Memories of their last conversation raced through his mind. Did her absence signal a change of heart?

The judge strode to his chair and collapsed into it, allowing everyone else to settle into their chairs. His stern face pierced the courtroom with an air of authority.

Words were exchanged that Grant barely heard. Mitchell rose next to him, making a motion to dismiss the case on insufficient evidence.

"Your Honor, we are just beginning to explore the newest

physical evidence; however, the case we've already built against the defendant is solid."

The judge shuffled through papers as the DA continued his defense of his case. "The defendant has a reputation, Your Honor. In fact, not more than twelve hours ago, he lunged at one of my own detectives for making a remark about his wife. We've got the right guy."

"My client's reputation is not grounds for a first-degree murder charge. The prosecution's evidence is circumstantial at best."

"We didn't need a body to discern what happened to Evelyn Clarke. On top of that, the defendant has no alibi."

"Enough," the judge said, holding up a hand. "Mr. Caldwell, do you have supporting evidence for your motion?"

"I do, Your Honor." Mitchell strode forward, handing off his paperwork before he thrust a copy toward the DA.

Grant pushed his mind to focus, trying to read the judge's face as he read through the information. Behind him, Sierra's phone buzzed. He shot a glance over his shoulder as she read her display and swiped to take the call, hurrying out of the room.

He swore he heard her hiss, "Where are you?"

Was it Julia? The judge's gaze lingered on the papers, the room thick with anticipation. Grant's fingers tapped a nervous rhythm on the table, his eyes darting toward the door with a mix of hope and dread.

"I'm prepared to make my ruling."

"WHAT?!"

Sierra's shrill voice sounded through the door from the hall. She burst into the courtroom, her expression a dramatic blend of urgency and triumph.

She pushed through the wooden swing gate and flung her arm in the air, clutching her phone like a trophy.

"Stop everything."

The judge furrowed his brow as Grant's heart sank. This would not bode well for his case.

"Miss Harrington, this is highly irregular. I will have order in this Court."

"Sierra, sit down," Mitchell hissed.

"I have groundbreaking information critical to this case. On this call is my stepmother, Julia Stanton Harrington. Julia, would you please tell the court what you just told me?" Sierra raised her eyebrows as she waited.

Grant's heart thudded in his chest.

Julia?

The courtroom fell into a hushed, tense silence. The judge leaned forward, intrigued but skeptical.

Julia's voice sounded through the tiny speaker, filling the courtroom as a siren rang out in the background. "Evelyn Clarke is alive. I'm with her right now."

Grant's heart skipped a beat, a variety of emotions swirling. Was it possible? Could Evelyn be alive? Hope and fear cascaded through him, along with a looming question of what this meant moving forward.

Gasps rose from others in the courtroom as the news broke.

"Your Honor," the DA shouted, "you cannot possibly be falling for this little stunt pulled by the defense."

"We had nothing to do with this. This is new information to us, too," Mitchell said.

The judge narrowed his eyes at Sierra as she refused to look away, her face frozen in a triumphant smile. "I can assure you this is no stunt. This is breaking information from a woman who would not lie."

"Would not lie? She's married to the defendant!" the DA shouted. "This reeks of a desperate attempt to buy time on the defense's part."

"Oh, this is hardly desperate," Sierra said as the display on her phone changed to a video chat. The camera bobbled around for a moment before it focused on the frail form of Evelyn Clarke, clinging to someone as she squinted against the bright morning sun.

Sierra's grin widened as the proof bloomed on her screen. She spun the phone for everyone to see.

"There we have it. Proof."

She shot a coy glance at the DA. "You may want to check your sources again, because it looks like whatever body you dug up has nothing to do with this case."

"Mr. Donovan, would you like a brief recess to consult with your sources before you move forward with these charges?" the judge asked.

He rubbed his ashen complexion as he bobbed his head. "Yes, Your Honor," he said, his voice barely above a whisper before he stumbled through the swinging gate and hurried from the courtroom, fumbling with his phone.

Sierra finally lowered the phone, but before Grant could follow up with her about any of the shocking information they'd just heard, the DA returned to the courtroom. He strode to his table, balancing his fingers against it, his eyes staring at the floor as he moved his colorless lips.

"Your Honor, at this time, the prosecution would like to withdraw all charges against the defendant, pending further investigation."

The judge bobbed his head as he slammed down the gavel. "Mr. Harrington, you are free to go."

Grant flicked his gaze to his legal counsel. "Is that it? Is it really over?"

"It is. For this round. I'll keep my ear to the ground for anything else looming. But for now, you're free to go."

Grant grinned at the news as he rose from his chair and stuck his hand out to shake his attorney's.

"Yay, Daddy!" Sierra said with a clap of her hands before she wrapped her arms around his neck.

He pulled back. "Is Julia still on the line?"

"No, call dropped."

"Where is she? Is she okay?"

"She seemed okay. I'll try to call her again." Sierra tapped on her phone and waited as it rang, going to voicemail again. "Seriously? You call and drop a bombshell like that, then you don't pick up?"

"Try again. We have to find her." Grant's stomach gnawed as the high of his win waned, replaced with concern for his wife.

"Let me see if I can get any information from the police. They owe us at this point."

Mitchell stepped away to have a word with the DA as he packed papers in his briefcase. Sierra tried Julia's phone again but received only her voicemail. She stamped a foot on the floor, with a muffled scream.

"I don't like this," Grant said, tension building in his shoulders.

Mitchell returned and hauled his briefcase off the table. "Let's head over to dispatch. They should be receiving the information firsthand."

"No," Grant said, with a shake of his head. "I want her location. We'll go straight there."

"They're not going to give us that. It's likely going to be closed as a crime scene."

Grant gave his legal counsel an icy stare, his voice disapproving. "Mitchell–"

"Let's get our bearings with dispatch and go from there. The last thing we need is another charge. The DA is reeling, but that won't last for long."

Grant heaved a sigh, gritting his teeth. He didn't like to be out of control in a situation that affected someone important to him. But with no other options, he followed his attorney, exiting into the bright morning sun to cross to the police station.

Within a few minutes, they stood in the dispatch office behind one of the dispatchers in contact with the officers on the scene.

"Request status from the scene," the dispatcher said.

A second later, the radio crackled to life as an officer's voice filled the air. "Bus requested for sixty-two-year-old female vic with multiple injuries. Vic is alert and responsive at this time."

Usually composed yet dramatic, Sierra clasped a hand around her father's arm, her eyes shining with an uncharacteristic vulnerability. "Sounds like Evelyn is okay."

"Yeah," Grant answered, his mind going to the other woman at the scene. "What about the others there? My wife is there. Julia."

"Ten-twenty-seven, requesting status for second female on scene. Julia Harrington."

Grant held his breath, awaiting the confirmation that she was okay.

The officer's voice responded a moment later. "Alert and responsive, with multiple injuries. Ambulance requested. Paramedics arriving on scene now."

His heart lurched at the words, his chest tightening. "Where are they?"

Mitchell held up a hand to silence Grant.

"Mitch, I want to know where she is. How extensive are her injuries?"

Mitchell bobbed his head up and down as he addressed the dispatcher. "Are they sending her to a hospital?"

"Ten-twenty-seven, request destination for second female vic."

Grant slid his hands to his hips as he bit into his lower lip, his heart still pounding against his ribs.

"Dispatch, both vics en route to St. Mary's Memorial."

The news finally gave him an actionable result. "St. Mary's, let's go."

"Thank you for your help," Mitchell said as Grant hurried from the room.

"We can walk from here," Grant said, his steps quick with the urgency of determining the extent of his wife's injuries, and his secretary's.

"Daddy, slow down!" Sierra said, with a scoff. "I'm calling James. He can drive us."

She froze as his phone went to voicemail before she hurried after her father.

"It's not that far, Sierra, we'll walk. By the time James gets here, we could be there."

"Fine," she said, with a groan. "But you're paying for my foot massage."

"Done," he said as they hit the sidewalk and aimed for the hospital across town, arriving in the chaotic emergency room fifteen minutes later.

Grant dodged a few people, trying to get to the admissions desk to ask about Julia, his frustration growing with every step.

"Mr. Harrington!" a familiar voice called from behind him.

He twisted, finding James rising from a seat and waving.

Grant crossed to him with Sierra in tow. "James, what are you doing here?"

"I was with Mrs. Harrington at the warehouse where we found Mrs. Clarke."

Grant's heart skipped a beat. "What the hell happened?" His next words lingered on his lips, but he wasn't sure he could get them out. His voice faltered, his tone low. "How hurt is she?"

James flicked his gaze away from Grant, a move that suggested to Grant that he wouldn't like the answer he was about to get. "They're doing some tests now, uh…"

"Tests? James, what happened?"

The man's shoulders slumped ever so slightly, betraying a feeling of guilt.

"James?"

James pressed his lips together as he shook his head. "I should have stayed with her, we split up…"

"James, what happened to her?" He tried to keep his voice as even-toned as possible.

James breathed out a shaky breath. "She took a pretty hard hit. But she was speaking clearly, she wasn't disoriented…"

"Hit from what? Did she fall?"

James heaved a sigh. "No. Someone was there."

"Someone attacked her?" he cried, feeling his chest tightened again.

"Yeah. He got away, but not before he…did some damage."

Grant rubbed his face as he sank into a chair. What had he gotten this poor woman into? And how would she react after having lived through what surely was the worst week of her life?

James eased onto the seat across from him. "She seemed okay. She was talking, walking. She seemed fine."

Grant gripped the arm of the chair as he sought to rein in his tension. "What were you doing there?"

"Mrs. Harrington woke me up early this morning and said she found some sort of clue. Something about the donor list."

Grant let his head fall back between his shoulder blades.

She'd moved on the donor list herself after he was arrested. He should have told her not to do anything herself.

"She insisted on going. She said she'd go without me if I didn't take her."

"Of course she did," Grant answered with a shake of his head as someone called his name.

He rose from his seat and crossed to the scrubs-clad woman, with Sierra and James in tow. "You can follow me," she said.

They wandered past rows of filled beds separated by curtains. His stomach knotted as he wondered what he would find when he arrived at her bedside. Would she prefer not to see him?

"...told you I'm fine," her voice floated toward him, making him quicken his steps. "I feel fine."

The woman in scrubs pulled the curtain back slightly and motioned for them to enter. Grant raced through the opening, his eyes wide as he studied her. Her normally pale features seemed a little paler, and her eyes looked tired. A surge of protectiveness coursed through him, mingled with guilt for pulling her into this world.

The doctor tapped on a tablet next to her. Julia flicked her gaze to him, the familiar tiny smile curling her lips. "Hi."

He breathed a sigh of relief as he closed the gap between them and took her hand. "What did you think you were doing?"

"Getting a severe concussion," the doctor answered for her.

"Does she need to stay?" Grant asked.

"No," Julia answered. "She does not. She is fine."

"She is able to go home if she promises to rest. Close monitoring for the next forty-eight hours. You'll want to watch for signs of confusion, seizures, vomiting, weakness, or numbness in her arms and legs, slurred speech, or worsening of her headache. It's normal to have a pretty severe headache after a hit to the head like Mrs. Harrington sustained, but if it becomes unbearable, you need to return her to the emergency room immediately."

The doctor tapped the tablet again. "Strict rest, no activities that could result in another hit on the head, and nothing taxing mentally. No long hours on the computer, reading, or anything like that. Just rest."

Julia heaved a sigh at the long list of restrictions as Grant nodded. "Absolutely. She will not move out of her bed for the next forty-eight hours, Doctor, I promise you."

"Good. I'll send the nurse in with the discharge papers." The doctor pressed the tablet to her chest as she left the curtained-off area.

Grant glanced down at Julia, shifting a lock of her hair to expose a cut on her forehead. "Are you okay?"

She squeezed his hand and offered him a weak smile. "Yes. I am. I'm fine. How are you? What happened in court?"

He couldn't stop a chuckle from escaping his lips. As she lay in a hospital bed, her first concern was him. "The charges were dropped."

"Good. And have you heard anything about Evelyn?"

"Not yet. I'll check before we go. You were my first concern. Julia, you shouldn't have done this alone."

"I didn't," she said, with a shake of her head. "I took James."

"James," Grant said, keeping his voice measured, "never should have agreed to take you to that warehouse."

"We had to do something."

"And now you're going to do nothing for the next two days."

"But there is still so much to figure out," Julia pleaded. "We found Evelyn, but who would have taken her, and why?"

"Those are all questions we will find answers to, but not while you're recovering from a concussion."

Julia tugged one corner of her lips back in silent disagreement, but the arrival of the nurse halted any further conversation. After a repeat of all the instructions, they discharged her.

"Do you want to visit Evelyn?" Julia asked as she climbed from the bed.

"No, I want to take you home and make sure you're okay."

"I'm fine. I–"

"Am going home right now. I think you've had enough excitement for one day."

They waited in the crisp morning air, the sun casting long shadows across the pavement while James brought the car around. They slipped inside, the leather seats cool against their skin, and arrived home forty-five minutes later. The tension in Grant's shoulders eased as they stepped through the door into the quiet house.

Worthington met them at the door. "Mrs. Harrington, we are so pleased to have you home."

"Thank you," she said, with a demure smile.

"And now straight to bed," Grant insisted.

"I thought that was all just for the doctor's benefit."

Grant arched an eyebrow. "No, it was not. To bed, Julia."

Julia heaved a sigh as she climbed the stairs. Grant watched her go, a mix of admiration and something else he couldn't quite admit to himself yet. But the ordeal had managed to pull back some of the layers he'd built up over the years. Or rather, Julia had done that. And he wasn't certain he could deny that he cared for her much longer.

"What can I do for you, Mr. Harrington? Would you like your phone or briefcase?"

"I need to call Mitchell. I want him following up on what happened to Evelyn."

"Yes, sir." Worthington crossed to his office, with Grant following. "And afterward?"

"Afterwards, I'm going to make sure Julia does what the doctor ordered. I don't want her sitting alone after what she went through."

Worthington bobbed his head as he dialed the number for Mitchell Caldwell and handed the phone to Grant.

"If you're calling about following up on Evelyn, I'm already on that," Mitchell answered. "Not much information just yet, but I am keeping a pulse on this investigation."

"Good. I'll pass along any information that led Julia to find her as soon as I have it. Otherwise, I will see you tomorrow at the board meeting."

"Well, I've got a nice surprise for you. That's been canceled since the charges were dropped. They still want to review your performance, but with the recent developments, no one's going to push this right now."

The corner of Grant's lips turned up. It seemed they'd dodged one bullet. Perhaps the tides were turning.

"Keep me up-to-date."

Grant replaced the receiver and loosened his tie as he left the office behind and climbed the stairs, navigating the halls to Julia's suite. He couldn't stop the grin from spreading across his face. Light shined at the end of the tunnel in terms of keeping his company intact and under his control.

And he couldn't deny the growing feelings he had for his new wife. Marrying her just may have been the best decision he'd ever made.

CHAPTER 24

JULIA

*J*ulia squeezed her eyes closed, swallowing hard as the MRI whirred around her. Without any visual cues anchoring her to the world, her mind regressed to the warehouse.

She hadn't seen her attacker fast enough, too stunned by the discovery of Evelyn Clarke. By the time she turned, the bat he carried had smacked her right in the temple.

It had been all she could do to stay conscious. After the hit blurred her vision, she wanted to collapse on the floor and curl into a ball, but she couldn't give in.

"Doing great, Mrs. Harrington, just another minute," a voice said from a speaker in the machine, jarring her back to reality, but only for an instant.

She recalled stumbling to the wall and whipping around to face her attacker. With a cocky swagger, he'd stalked forward toward her, tapping the bat off his opposite hand.

His face, covered with a ski mask, still allowed his wicked grin to show through.

Tears streamed down both her and Evelyn's cheeks as the man cornered her. He swung, but Julia dodged him at the last second, her head splitting with every movement.

The sound of the bat cracking off the cement block wall made it worse. She slipped under his arms and stumbled a few steps forward before spinning to keep her eye on him.

He growled as he whipped around to face her again. She shuffled backward as he swung at her again.

"Run, Julia!" Evelyn shouted.

"No," Julia huffed. "I'm not leaving you."

"Looks like you both die, then," the man growled. This time, he aimed his bat at Evelyn.

With a shriek, Julia plowed into his side before he could swing. She drove him back against the wall. He threw her off easily, knocking her to the ground.

Her temples pounded as she tried to climb to her feet, but he reached her first. With a swift kick, he sent her rolling across the floor again.

She landed in a heap, with a groan. He stalked across the room as she flopped onto her back. Her eyes filled with tears as he lowered his toes onto her wrist, pinning her to the ground.

His lips pulled back into another vicious grin as he raised his bat overhead.

"Hey!" a voice barked from behind him.

The man froze and swung his gaze behind him. Gunfire echoed, and a bullet slammed into her attacker's shoulder.

The pressure let off her wrist as he stumbled back, dropping the bat and grabbing his shoulder. Blood oozed through between his fingers.

James inched into the door, his gun still pointed at the assailant. The man lunged sideways, and James fired again.

This time, the bullet smacked into the wall. The attacker scrambled for the door and disappeared through it.

James raced toward her. "Mrs. Harrington? You okay?"

"Yeah," she groaned as she pushed up to sitting.

"Did he hurt you?"

She pressed her fingers to the sticky blood soiling her hair. "He hit me."

"Can you walk?"

"Yeah," she said as he helped her to her feet. "We need to get her out of here. She needs medical attention."

"I can't believe she's alive." James shoved the gun into his waistband before he flicked open a pen knife and cut Evelyn's bonds before scooping her up to carry her from the building.

Julia dug her phone from her pocket and keyed in 911 before she pressed it to her ear. She gave their location and information to the dispatcher, hanging up as they hurried out into the morning sun. James sat Evelyn in the back seat of the SUV as Julia placed another call.

She drummed her fingers against her thigh, shifting her weight back and forth as the line trilled.

"Mrs. Harrington, you should sit down," James whispered, guiding her to the front seat.

"Where are you?" Sierra's voice hissed at her in greeting.

"Sierra, I'm sorry I'm not there, but you must listen. Evelyn Clarke is alive. We are with her now. She's okay, we're waiting for the police and ambulance."

"WHAT?!" Sierra exclaimed. "Wait, hold on."

Julia tightened her grip on the phone as Sierra's voice sounded on the other end of the line. "Stop everything!"

The MRI finally whirred down, and the table slid out of the machine, breaking the memory of the dramatic reveal.

"How did it look?" Julia asked as they wheeled her back down to the emergency room. "Do I still have a brain?"

The transport woman chuckled at her as she tugged the bed back into the small stall. "Doctor will be with you shortly."

She pulled the curtain closed around her, leaving Julia alone to wait. She clasped and unclasped her hands as she waited alone for the results. The experience had been surreal. She still wondered if it had been real.

Had she really found Evelyn Clarke alive?

It fueled in her the need to dig deeper. Who had done this? Who would have kidnapped this woman, and faked her death? And why?

There was so much more to this story.

Her thoughts were interrupted by the arrival of a scrub-clad doctor, carrying a tablet. She tapped around on it before she flicked her gaze to Julia.

"Good morning, Mrs. Harrington. I'm Dr. Vanessa Reynolds. It sounds like you've had quite an eventful morning."

"Unfortunately, yes," Julia said. "But I feel okay. When can I go home?"

"We'll see about that," the doctor said, returning her gaze to the tablet. "I've got your results here."

Julia swallowed hard, waiting to determine if there had been some damage from the attack. She desperately hoped there wasn't. She needed a functioning mind to keep writing.

"Your MRI looks good. No bleeding or swelling."

Julia blew out a sigh of relief at the news. "Good. So, can I go?"

The doctor chuckled at her. "Not quite yet. I'd like to do an exam and ask you a few questions. Do you still have a headache?"

"Uh, yes. It's not terrible."

"It's okay if it is," Dr. Reynolds said. "We just want to be sure we diagnose and treat you properly. So, can you tell me on a scale of one to ten how bad your pain is right now?"

"A six," Julia answered, with a slight shrug.

"Okay." The doctor removed a penlight from her pocket and clicked it on, flicking it into Julia's eyes. "Your pupils are equal and reactive, which is a good thing. Can you follow my finger?"

Julia shifted her eyes back and forth as the doctor trailed her finger through the air.

"Very good. Now, when you got hit, did you see stars?"

"Yes," Julia admitted, "but I don't anymore."

"Any blurred vision? Then or now?"

"Just a second after I got hit, but not now. My vision is clear."

"Nausea?"

Julia shook her head. "I told you I'm fine. I feel fine."

The curtain around her stall slid back, and Grant appeared, his eyes wide. His usual composed demeanor had been replaced by a look that hinted at genuine worry. Was his sudden concern genuine, or a facade?

She was surprised to see him out of court. This was likely a chunk out of his day he didn't need after that fiasco.

Behind him were James and Sierra. Julia stared at them for an extra second, the thought that they were seeing each other racing through her mind before she flicked her gaze to Grant and offered him a slight smile.

"Hi."

Grant heaved a sigh as he approached her and grabbed her hand. "What did you think you were doing?"

The doctor answered him, though Julia insisted she was fine. And after a laundry list of instructions and warning signs, all of which Grant agreed to, doing well in his role of doting husband, they agreed to discharge her.

Julia sighed, glad she would be returning home as Grant slid a lock of her hair aside, pinching the cut on her head.

"Are you okay?" he asked.

Julia squeezed his hand and smiled. She much preferred to find out if what they'd been through resulted in good news, though she assumed with Grant being at the hospital, things had gone well.

"I'm fine. How are you? What happened in court?"

He chuckled at her before he told her the charges were dropped. She heaved another sigh of relief before she asked about Evelyn.

"Not yet. I'll check before we go. You were my first concern. Julia, you shouldn't have done this alone."

"I didn't," she said, with a shake of her head. "I took James."

Annoyance crept into his voice as he said, "James never should have taken you there."

"We had to do something." Julia defended their actions.

"And now you're going to do nothing for the next two days."

"But there is still so much to figure out," Julia pleaded. "We found Evelyn, but who would have taken her, and why?"

"Those are all questions we will find answers to, but not while you're recovering from a concussion."

Her discharge papers finally arrived, and she inched closer to going home. They waited in the bright morning sunshine for James to bring the car around after she asked Grant about seeing Evelyn.

Within forty-five minutes, they arrived at Harrington House. Her headache seemed to ease slightly as the quiet house surrounded them.

Worthington met them at the door. "Mrs. Harrington, we are so pleased to have you home."

"Thank you," she answered.

"And now straight to bed," Grant insisted.

Julia shot him a surprised glance. "I thought that was all just for the doctor's benefit?"

Grant arched an eyebrow. "No, it was not. To bed, Julia."

With a sigh, she climbed the stairs, leaving everyone behind. Perhaps it wouldn't be so bad to spend the day in bed. Better now with a staff of servants than a year from now, when she'd be on her own again and dishes would pile up or she'd go hungry.

And she could work from her bed. She changed her clothes into something comfortable, grabbed her laptop, and climbed into her bed.

Evelyn's rescue had closed one chapter, but they stood at the start of a deeper mystery. Who was behind it all? And what else did they have planned?

The idea of tracking down more information forced her to pull her laptop onto her lap. It distracted her from the idea that one year from now, her life would revert back to normal. As the day's events washed over her, she recalled her fear, adrenaline, and now a strange sense of belonging. She'd come to care for these people more than she'd expected. She'd miss them. She'd probably miss one person the most.

She shoved the idea from her head as a knock sounded at the door. She called out, expecting Worthington to be checking on her or bringing her a cup of tea.

Instead, a voice scolded her. "Julia, nothing taxing."

She glanced at him as he crossed the room and pushed the laptop closed. With a frown, she said, "This shouldn't wait."

"Mitchell is following up."

"He doesn't know everything. He doesn't know how we found that warehouse. And I think that's important."

"I'm sure it is," Grant answered as he grabbed the laptop and crossed the room, dumping it on a side table well outside of her current reach. She'd have to go all the way across the room to retrieve it when he left.

"And what about the board meeting tomorrow?"

Grant tugged his tie looser and slipped it from around his neck, tossing it on the armchair. "Canceled. With the charges dropped, no one wanted to move forward with it."

"Oh, that's good news." She wondered if maybe she'd be moving back to her apartment sooner than a year from now.

"Which still leaves us plenty of work, but none of it has to be done now." He slid off his jacket and tossed it aside. "Which means I can take time to make sure you're following the doctor's instructions."

Her features pinched at the words. "I don't need a babysitter."

He tossed his cufflinks on the table and rolled up his sleeves. "Apparently, you do. You weren't left alone for five minutes before you were trying to work."

"Life doesn't stop when you're sick."

"For you, it does."

She narrowed her eyes at him, unable to figure out why he insisted on staying. "Don't you have work to do?"

"Are you trying to get rid of me?"

"I'm just saying that I'm fine. You don't have to sit here with me."

He crossed to her and eased onto the edge of the bed. "Julia, you went through a lot today. I want to stay. I want to make sure you're okay."

She stared up at him, her forehead creasing. Something about the way he looked at her made her wonder if…she quickly dismissed it. They had a professional relationship.

"Okay," she said, her voice softer than she'd intended.

"Good," he said with a grin as he rose and strode around the bed, settling onto the other side. "I was beginning to think you didn't like me."

Julia stared at him, a confused smile crossing her features.

Grant kicked off his shoes as he leaned back into the pillows. "You know, we really make a pretty good team."

Her smile broadened. "I do have a knack for getting you out of trouble."

His eyes sparkled at her. "Yes, you do, Julia."

Whatever happened as they faced the problems at Harrington Global, she supposed it would be an interesting year. But they'd face it together.

The End
To be continued…

<u>Want to Read More About Grant and Julia?</u>
Read *Blackmail of a Billionaire*

**Grant's a hard-headed CEO.
But He's Never Negotiated For His Wife's Life.**

Julia knew marrying Billionaire CEO, Grant Harrington, was never going to be easy. Keeping the "fake" part of their marriage under wraps until his board of directors backs off —that's the ultimate challenge.

She's been contracted to clean up Grant's image and create a stable home at Harrington House—easier said than done. Especially as Grant's daughter, Sierra, who's got more issues than Time magazine.

Julia's natural charm works on just about everybody, and Grant's job is looking safer by the minute. His feelings for her? That's where lines blur. Their marriage contract is crystal clear—it's strictly business. Yet Julia has become more than just a prop.

Julia knows her marriage is fake. That doesn't stop her caring about Grant and his daughter—maybe more than she should. So when she's kidnapped along with Sierra, she'll do anything to get them both home safe.

Grant is used to the high-stakes world of business. But he's about to find out that love is the riskiest game of all.

Find out what happens in *Blackmail of a Billionaire* available on Amazon now! Click HERE to get your copy!

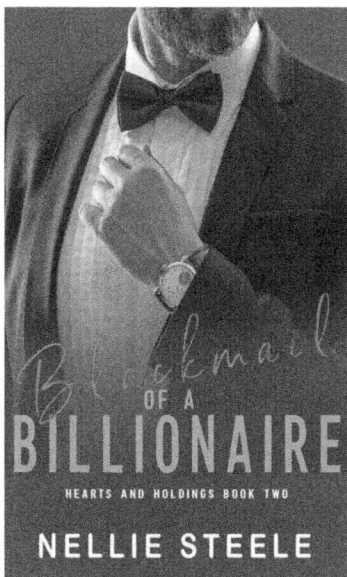

Click HERE to get your copy of Blackmail of a Billionaire

Let's keep in touch! Join my newsletter!

SERIES BY NELLIE STEELE

Hearts and Holdings

Bet on a Billionaire

Blackmail of a Billionaire

Bargain with a Billionaire

Battle with a Billionaire

Betrayal of a Billionaire

Bluff by a Billionaire

Believing in a Billionaire

Bliss with a Billionaire

ABOUT THE AUTHOR

Award-winning author Nellie Steele writes in as many genres as she reads, ranging from romance to fantasy and allowing readers to escape reality and enter enchanting worlds filled with unique, lovable characters.

Addicted to books since she could read, Nellie escaped to fictional worlds like the ones created by Carolyn Keene or Victoria Holt long before she decided to put pen to paper and create her own realities.

When she's not crafting a new romance yarn, spinning a cozy mystery tale, building a new realm in a contemporary fantasy, or writing another action-adventure car chase, you can find her shuffling through her Noah's Ark of rescue animals or enjoying a hot cuppa (that's tea for most Americans.)

Join the Hearts of Steele Romance Readers' Group on Facebook!

Made in the USA
Las Vegas, NV
07 February 2025

17545035R00144